THE HADFIELD SERIES

REVEALING A ROGUE

TEMPTING A GENTLEMAN

LOVING A DOWAGER

First Edition November 2021

Developmental Edit by Gray Plume Editing

Edited by Rare Bird Editing

Proofread by Magnolia Author Services

Cover design by The Swoonies Book Covers

Copyright © 2021 by Rachel Ann Smith

ISBN 978-1-951112-14-1

LOVING A DOWAGER

RACHEL ANN SMITH

PENFORD
PUBLISHING

AUTHOR'S NOTE

Dear Readers,

Writing the Hadfields, and especially *Loving a Dowager*, has been a rollercoaster. I write all my books with the intention of providing readers with a few hours of escape into my fictional regency word.

I titled Henrietta's book well before I started drafting her story. If you Google "dowager" it is defined as *a widow with a title or property derived from her late husband*. While Henrietta was technically entitled to keep her title of "Lady," being a daughter of a duke, she had been disowned by her family. In addition, she married George, a younger son of an earl who never inherited the title, which meant she would in fact not be considered a dowager. I admit I've taken the liberty of using the informal definition of dowager, *a dignified elderly woman*, in titling Henrietta's story.

I appreciate the time you spend with my fictional charac-
ters and made-up world.

Happy Reading,

Rachel Ann

ACKNOWLEDGMENTS

Writing historical romance novels has opened up my world far beyond what I believed possible.

I am forever grateful to all the readers who have embraced my fictional regency world filled with agents from the Home Office, Foreign Office, Protectors of the Royal Family (PORF's), and the Network.

I want to thank my newsletter subscribers, who provided me with a wonderful selection of possible names and voted to determine the gender of the newest member of the Drummond family. A special thanks to Deana Dent, who voted for a baby girl and suggested the beautiful name Abigail. Lady Abigail Drummond will have her very own story in the future.

Without the support and patience of my husband, my children, my critique partner, my editorial team, my fellow authors, my cover artist, and my virtual assistant, none of my stories would be published. And if it weren't for you, my readers, I would have to go back to being an accountant and crunch numbers again, so a huge "Thank you" for continuing to purchase and delve into my made-up regency world.

LOVING A DOWAGER

*H*enrietta Neale's heels hit the polished wooden floors of Neale & Sons with a regimented click-clack. The tempo of her footsteps echoed the urgency of the matter at hand. In no mood for idle chatter, Henrietta was intent on speaking to the man her second son, Christopher, left in charge of her deceased husband's law firm. Lord Walter Weathersbee. The warm smiles from the staff were replaced with furrowed brows as they caught sight of the determined set of her normally friendly features. It was her first appearance at the firm since Walter assumed role as principal.

A few feet from her destination, Henrietta grumbled, "Of all the qualified applicants, Christopher had to choose the most pedantic fellow I know." Her sons might well believe Walter capable of running Neale & Sons, but she knew better. Lord Walter Weathersbee, four years her junior and the third son of a marquise, was nothing like her deceased husband George Neale, and she would not allow the man to destroy the legacy George had worked so hard to establish and her sons to maintain.

She pushed open his office door and marched up to stand before Walter. The massive hardwood desk that once belonged to George stretched between them. With her hands firmly planted on her hips, she stared down at the man who used to trail her about her papa's estate. "Pray tell, why did you decline Lady Bertha as a client of Neale & Sons?"

Walter removed his spectacles and stood, forcing her to tilt up her chin. He was no longer a lanky lad barely an inch or two taller than her. "How kind of you, Henrietta, to come for a visit." He motioned for her to take a seat as he sank back into his own chair.

Unwilling to relinquish her position, she remained standing. Oh, how she wished she had need of a cane. A woman of her years should have a cane. Then she could use it to whack the insolent young pup over the head. She glared at the man before her. Silver strands weaved through his chestnut hair. A quick simple calculation reminded her Walter was seven-and-forty. Studying him closer revealed that Walter was no longer the doe-eyed pup of their youth but a rather dashing gentleman. The man's lips curved into a smile, provoking a long-forgotten fluttering in her chest. A multitude of questions raced through her mind as to why she would experience such a reaction to the man who was once a boon companion.

Henrietta reorganized her thoughts back to the matter at hand. She needed to convey to Walter that neither George nor her sons would ever turn away a woman in need of legal representation. No. George had been a firm believer that women should have control of their own assets. Until this day, she'd had no need to invoke her rights as fifty percent share owner in the firm. Her sons fully understood her stance on the firm's policy to defend and protect women's interests. A position she would have to make clear to the man whose gaze was fully trained upon her.

Slightly bent at the waist, Henrietta huffed. "That scoundrel and fortune hunter, Lord Otterman, is taking advantage of my friend." Had she not still been suffering from the effects of his smile, she might have begun with a more informative and appropriate opening statement.

Walter lowered his hands that had been clasped beneath his chin. "So you said in your missive to me yesterday. And as instructed, I paid a visit to Lady Bertha, who informed me she was in no need of my services. The lady claims her impending nuptials are the result of a love match." He motioned to the empty chair next to her. "Please, have a seat."

She didn't intend to stay long, but it would be rude to remain standing. She slipped into the chair, mentally reassuring herself her decision to sit had nothing to do with the buckling of her knees at the sight of his lopsided grin.

After smoothing out her skirts, she faced Walter once

more. "Bah. Bertha is still an innocent despite her having reached the age of nine-and-forty. She has never been truly courted before. Otterman's only interest in Bertha is her recent inheritance—a healthy sum, from what she has shared with me. The cad is a fortune hunter; he's not in love with her."

Henrietta's palms began to sweat as fears from her youth resurfaced. Daughter of a duke, her dowry had been substantial. The summer leading up to her debut, she had agonized with a younger version of the man seated opposite her. Walter clearly had forgotten her abhorrence of men like Otterman.

"Are you certain? Otterman has yet to sire an heir. Offering to marry a woman past her prime childbearing years is proof enough for me the man is in love."

"Good gracious, spoken like a confirmed bachelor. What would you know of love? You've never married."

Walter's brows knitted for a brief moment before returning to their neutral state. He was never skilled at masking his reactions; at least, not that she could recall. "That I never married does not mean I've never been in love," he replied.

"If that is true, then you are a fool not to have offered for the woman's hand." Henrietta sat back and waited for Walter to object. The man was no fool. Even when he had but fourteen years on this earth, he was the only person of her acquaintance who could drive her to distraction with his clever word play—until she met and fell in love with George. Tapping her toe against the leg of her chair, she counted to thirty. "What? No clever retort this time?"

Sunlight glinted off his spectacles as they swung from side to side. "You, my dear, are correct. I should have informed my lady love of my interest, but by the time I had gathered enough courage to do so, she was no longer available to my suit."

His intense stare left an unsettled feeling in her tightly corseted chest. She had long ago dispensed with the need to fidget under another's gaze. Yet resisting the urge to shift in her seat was fast becoming a challenge. Memories of Walter making her laugh and the freedom she felt in his company flooded her mind. She smiled, recalling their brisk early morning rides. Racing across their family estates before they were forced inside to begin their daily routines. His in the schoolroom with a tutor and hers stuck in the drawing room learning idiotic skills that were expected of an accomplished lady, like painting with watercolors or how to sit with an artificial smile. Activities she abandoned the day she married George. Her heart ached as another memory came to the forefront: her wedding, a simple but love-filled ceremony held at Hadfield Hall some thirty-plus years ago.

Walter cleared his throat, bringing her focus back to the present. She stared at the mature, composed, handsome man before her. Banished were the images of the boy she had secretly wished was a year or two older than herself. She focused on the fine lines about his eyes and his lips. This older version of Walter Weathersbee was wreaking havoc on her normally steady pulse. Heat warmed her cheeks. What had they been discussing?

Love. His missed opportunity. Tugging at the fingertips of gloves, she blurted, "How is it that you did not find another to love? With so many men lost or at war, surely there must have been a woman or two that caught your attention over the years."

"I could ask the same of you, Henrietta Neale. Your husband died at an early age. Why haven't you found another man to marry?"

Of course, Walter had to form the one counterargument that she wished to avoid. "When did you develop the habits of a barrister—answering a question with a question?"

"And again, I could ask the same of you." If she hadn't been watching him closely, she might have missed the slight twitch at the corner of his lips.

Infuriating man. As a boy, when she had challenged him, he would be the first to give in. Apparently over the years he'd developed a stubbornness. She wasn't sure if she liked or disliked this new trait of Walter's. She crossed her arms over her chest. "I had my hands full raising two boys."

"I understand."

He would. When her eldest son Landon had ascended to the title and been forced to enter the fray of the ton, she too made her reentrance into society. The matrons had been quick to update her on all the scandalous gossip now that she was once again, one of them. It had been nearly two decades since Walter's two older brothers and their wives had passed in a terrible carriage accident. Walter had undertaken their guardianship and the task of raising his two nephews and niece all on his own. The ton had been aghast all these years that he chose to care for the children rather than marry and provide the children with a mother.

An ache settled in the center of her chest. She hadn't shared the litany of fears that had prevented her from taking the risk to love once more. She wasn't ready to face them herself, let alone admit them to another. It stood to reason that Walter would also harbor reservations that prevented him from falling in love. Her intuition screamed that she was wrong—the Walter she had known was a passionate soul and more than capable of loving. But why had he remained a bachelor?

Agitated at the course of her thoughts, Henrietta rose out of her chair. "Walter Weathersbee, as principal of Neale and Sons, it is your duty to review the marriage agreements that the conniving Lord Otterman has had drawn up and ensure Lady Bertha's interests are protected."

Rising from his chair, he pressed his fingertips on the top of the desk. "Henrietta. I did not craft... nor did I vote upon the marriage laws... that dictate upon marriage a husband has every right..."

Throwing her arms in the air, she interrupted, "I don't care what the blasted law is! I'm asking you to make certain that Lady Bertha is well provided for." Counting to ten, in the hope of regaining her composure, she bowed her head and clasped her hands tightly behind her back.

His fingertips turned white. "Why are you asking this of me? Why not ask Landon to see to the matter?"

She raised her gaze to meet his. "Landon is no longer a barrister." She looked about the office. "Neale & Sons is still a law firm, is it not? I'm coming to you because I—no, Lady Bertha needs excellent legal representation. George entrusted the running of the firm to Landon, Landon granted it to Christopher, and Christopher has left it to you to oversee in his absence." Moisture welled at the corner of her eye at the mention of her second son. She had failed to extract a date of return from Christopher, and she wasn't entirely sure if she would ever see her baby boy again before she left this earth. After all, every day over fifty was a miracle. For heaven's sake, she'd outlived most of the women that she'd had her coming out with, and even fewer men in their set were of a similar age. Walter was one of the few that remained hale and hearty. He raked his fingers through a remarkably full head of hair.

Walter snatched up his spectacles and settled them back upon his nose. The glasswear made him appear older, somehow bridging the age difference between them. "I'll consider your request to review the marriage settlements." He sank back down into his seat.

He hadn't agreed as she'd hoped, but he also hadn't said no. "My thanks, Walter."

He ducked his head and peered at the thick file before him. Shuffling papers about, he was muttering quietly, but Henrietta was well versed in reading lips. Narrowing her gaze on his lips, she deciphered his nattering: *I should have simply said no. Say no to Henrietta. What a notion.*

He snorted and finally noticed that she remained in the room with him. "What the devil? Why are you still here?" His dark brows lowered. "It's not like you to dilly dally." Walter finally stood.

Henrietta debated whether or not to take a small step back to prevent him from towering over her. She leaned forward placing her palms flat on his desk. "Promise to have an answer for me by this eve."

Walter's eyes were drawn to her décolleté and widened until they were as large as two buttons. "I shall make no such promises." His Adam's apple bobbed. "I have much to consider."

Her heart warmed, recognizing the flicker of appreciation in his expression was for her. She'd been impartial to men for years, but the heat in Walter's gaze ... it reminded her of parts of herself she'd long ignored. Lowering her gaze slightly, she once again was mesmerized by his firm but inviting lips. What an absurd notion. Inviting lips, indeed! She found herself not only newly aware of her own desires, but of things that ignited them. Walter seemed a completely new man before her today. Henrietta quickly executed a curtsy that women half her age struggled to complete without falling to their knees. An image of her on the floor in front of Walter flashed before her. She hadn't a lurid thought in nearly two decades. In fact, too focused on ensuring the happiness and safety of others, she had not even considered or missed the gentle caresses nor the tantalizing feeling of a man inside her.

Walter had been spot on. She wasn't one to waste a moment. Preferred to always be on the go. If she stalled, her lingering fear of being unwanted, not needed, and cast aside once more might swallow her whole, and George wasn't here to save her this time. Solving one problem and then the next meant she need not face that dilemma. However, her boys were grown and happily married. They no longer needed her and she was desperate to fill that void, especially since Christopher's departure.

Hoping Walter hadn't read her mind like he easily had when they were younger, she straightened and said, "You are correct. There is much to consider. Are you attending the Redburns' ball this eve?"

"I shall make it a point to attend if that is where you will be." He walked out from behind the desk, closing the distance between them. A frisson in the air raised her senses. A magnetic pull she hadn't experienced since the last time she had been intimate with George erupted within her. But the sensation disappeared as quickly as it came as Walter strode past her and opened the door to the office for her to leave. Well. The gall of the man to kick her out of Neale & Sons.

"Henrietta, your cheeks are flushed, and I can see your breathing is slightly labored. Perhaps being in your deceased husband's office for an extended period has your nerves overwrought."

This. This is why the man remained a bachelor. The

man had not an inkling as to the cause of her discomfort, and she wasn't too keen to acknowledge the truth. It wasn't being in George's old office—it was Walter.

Stomping to the door, she stopped inches from him to say, "Thank you for explaining to me how I feel and what I'm experiencing. How did I exist all these years without you?"

Her comment garnered her a look from Walter she'd never seen on his features before. Hurt. Guilt. Anguish. A combination that transformed his handsome male features into a dark and brooding man who awakened feeling within Henrietta that she had firmly believed dead. With a quick nod, she left the building and entered the Hadfield coach awaiting her on the street.

Pressing her palms to her heated cheeks, Henrietta took in as much air as her lungs could accommodate and counted to ten. When had Walter Weathersbee transformed from the scraggly young lad who adored her like an older sister to the devilishly intense man who dared to challenge her and reignited dormant desires?

Since her reentrance into the social whirl of the ton two years ago, Henrietta had been well aware of Walter's shadowy presence at various events. She was always on alert and found having a familiar face in the crowd reassuring. On the rare occasion that they were within speaking distance, they had exchanged brief but pleasant greetings. Attributing the warmth that radiated in her chest when he was close to their past friendship, Henrietta was now faced with the reality the man increased not only her body temperature but the pace of her pulse. At the beginning of the season, Landon had shared with her his suspicion that Walter might hold a tendre for her after all these years. She had scoffed at the absurd idea but there was no denying the flicker of interest in Walter's gaze that had so weakened her, the need for a cane was real.

CHAPTER TWO

*S*lamming the thick file of information gathered on Lord Otterman closed, Walter grabbed his hat and coat off the stand beside the door. "Bloody troublesome women." He pulled out his pocket watch—fourteen past the hour. Where had the hours gone? If he wanted to get to the cemetery before Henrietta, he'd have to take a hack rather than walk.

As he marched towards the front entrance, the conspicuous stares from office staff increased his pace. Since Christopher's departure, Henrietta hadn't stepped foot into Neale & Sons. The staff were no doubt curious as to what prompted the woman's visit. Henrietta had no obvious ties to him, nor to any of the current cases that the firm was handling. Glaring back at them would do no good. Ignoring the overprotective bunch would be the best course of action. He slapped his hat on, tugged his gloves into place, and buttoned his coat that would hopefully ward off the chill outside. There was nothing he could do about the freezing glares he was leaving behind. Exiting through the front door, Walter waved down a hack.

"St. George's Gardens."

The driver nodded and pulled up the collar of his coat. Regularly visiting the grave of the deceased husband of the woman who owned your heart was hardly what one would call an act of romanticism. However, the increased number of reported cases of body snatching from the cemetery had led to Walter visiting George's grave on a weekly basis. Henrietta would be devastated if anything were to happen to George. Time had not weakened Henrietta's love for George, but it also hadn't weakened Walter's unrequited love for her. His frequent visits to his deceased friend had provided him an excuse to see Henrietta during the years she spent avoiding her ducal family. Since her return to society and residence in Mayfair, he had timed his visits to occur an hour before hers. Henrietta was a creature of habit, and once he ascertained her schedule, he adjusted his to accommodate his desire to see her on a regular basis. Today, however, he'd be lucky to arrive minutes before Henrietta. He still had to stop and purchase a bloom from the flower seller, ensure the trinket he'd brought was in place, and make his way to his hiding spot behind a large mausoleum which afforded the best viewing advantage.

The hack rolled to a stop. Walter jumped from the vehicle and flipped a crown up to the driver as he rushed to the corner.

A young woman held out a white bloom for him. "Yer

late and the lady's always bang up to the mark. Ye can give me yer gingerbread later."

He took the bloom without stopping. There was more in the air than the normal floral scent—a hint of... vanilla. Walter slowed and turned, narrowing his gaze upon the flower seller. With her hood pulled forward, her features were hidden, he returned to stand before her.

Frowning at the woman's bent head, Walter said, "I'll return and cough up the blunt. Don't leave." He noticed her petite, clean hands clenching the flower-filled basket she held close.

"Yer gonna be late."

She was right. Henrietta was never tardy. Rushing toward George's grave, he twisted to gain a glimpse of the woman who was posing as the regular flower seller, but the lady was gone. Yes, she had been a lady. The straight posture, the soft skin of her hands, the slight lilt in her tone, all were clues to her true identity. But why would a lady of the ton masquerade as a merchant? The trinket jingled against his palm. He needed to hurry. He'd have to puzzle out the identity of the woman later.

Walter scanned the area for any sign of Henrietta. The grave site was eerily quiet. No rustling of the leaves. The ground was wet from the recent rain, muffling the crunch of pebbles beneath his boots as he approached George's modest tombstone. He stuck the stem of the rose through the loop at the top of the charm he'd held in his palm. Kneeling, he gently laid the white flower on the ground. "By Jove, I think she'll cherish this charm just as she treasures all the memories you gave her, George."

He knelt for several breaths. He always, strangely, felt close to both George and Henrietta in these graveside moments. Grief and longing bound them all to one another. Booted heels crunched over fallen leaves. Damn. She'd arrived. Walter jumped to his feet and bolted, hiding behind the closest cemetery structure. It was barely large enough to conceal him. Two graves over, he was closer than he'd ever been before. Left with no choice, Walter hunkered down and waited.

Henrietta's sigh reached Walter's ears. "Well. Well. Well. George. The mystery of who has been leaving me trinkets over the years continues. Here I thought, it had been our sweet son, Christopher, the romantic. But the boy is an ocean away with his wife. Unless he devised some intricate plan and left these with another to leave for me, Christopher is not our mystery gift giver."

Walter closed his eyes and rested his head against the cold stone in front of him. All these years, the blasted woman thought his gifts had been from her youngest son. Of course she did. He'd never confessed his love for her. She had no clue how much she meant to him. He stopped breathing. Skirts rustled behind him. He turned to find Henrietta standing in the same pose she had earlier: hands firmly planted on her gently rounded hips, bent at the waist, affording him the most glorious view of the top of her bosom.

"Walter Weathersbee!"

At least Henrietta hadn't included his three middle names, like she used to when he was a lad. If she had, the severity of the situation would be tenfold. He stood and brushed off the crushed leaves from his coat.

When he met Henrietta's gaze, she asked, "What the devil are you doing here?"

The fire blazing in her eyes was a distraction. He hadn't been the recipient of such a look in years. In fact, no other woman had ever dared to look upon him with such... such passion. Now was not the time to dally about daydreaming of hauling Henrietta into his arms and stoking the flames he'd held banked for years.

Her brows that had initially shot up at the sight of him were drawn into a fierce scowl. Patience was not one of Henrietta's stronger suits. He'd better decide how to respond quickly. Before she resorted to his full name. He had two choices. Own up the fact he was responsible for the numerous heartfelt gifts he'd thought up over the years or allow Henrietta to believe Christopher had left instructions for him to see to this matter as he had with the law firm. He hadn't chosen to brazen it out with Henrietta when he was fourteen, but he was no longer that shy, innocent lad. He was older, wiser, and dammit—seven-and-forty. Puffing out his chest, he said, "I was visiting George."

"Why in the blazes are you visiting my late husband's grave?" She rolled her shoulders back, causing the material of her décolletage to stretch taut.

Heat rushed through Walter, which was doused by his words. "To pay my respects. It is, after all, the anniversary of George's death."

"But you weren't even acquainted with one another while George was alive."

It was one of the many secrets George and he had kept from Henrietta. "Ah, but we were." The fond memories of his bizarre arrangement with George had Walter chuckling. "We corresponded frequently. George had a fine mind and an unparalleled sense of humor. His advice was invaluable during my years at Eton and in my early years at Oxford prior to his death."

In all the years he'd known Henrietta, he'd never seen her at a loss for words. Yet here they stood staring at one another as dusk fell upon them. Henrietta continued to remain mute with her dark brows slashed downward to the center of her forehead, eyes narrowed, and soft moist lips slightly parted. He waited, letting the silence hang between them as he wrestled with the conflicting reactions of his body and his mind to the blush that had reached her cheeks.

Head cocked to one side, Henrietta asked, "Are you responsible for leaving me all the lovely charms over the years?"

Henrietta wasn't one to let matters lie. She'd get her answers one way or another.

"Yes." Time for more truths to be revealed. He took in a deep breath and continued, "As you know, George was an excellent chess player, always four steps ahead, always planning. He made me promise, in the event that he should leave this world, I was to do my best to make the day that marked his death something for you to look forward to and not dread. He was heartless in leaving me no clues how to fulfill my promise, but in his infinite wisdom he told me to remember what you love most. I remembered your love for mysteries, and so I created one just for you."

"So it wasn't Christopher who sent you here today. And it wasn't George who devised this scheme. It was all your doing?"

"Aye."

Confusion. Betrayal. And then something like delight flickered in Henrietta's eyes. She opened her clenched hand to reveal the trinket he'd left for her in the middle of her white-gloved palm. "Why did you decide upon a ship this year?"

"It was a salute to Christopher. I have faith he will return." The departure of Christopher and his new wife had been especially hard to watch from afar. Walter had wanted to be there standing next to her on the docks as she stood apart from the others and held back tears and waved her goodbyes.

"You don't know that for certain." She rolled the charm about in her hand. "Christopher will not be in Landon's shadow across the pond, and I know my dear boy has ambitions and talents that have nothing to do with his papa's chosen profession." Tears filled her eyes once more. Tears that would remain unshed because Henrietta Neale was not one to show the deep hurt that Walter knew she felt.

Hands slapped Walter's back, and before he could turn around to see who assaulted him, the stranger shoved him forward. Toward Henrietta. Her eyes widened and her arms shot out, catching him, stabilizing him. To his surprise, she rested her cheek against his chest and let the moisture seep into his coat. Glancing over his shoulder, he spied the worn but clean gray skirts he'd seen on the flower seller earlier. She wove between the cement blocks and then disappeared. No woman of his acquaintance moved with such speed and stealth. Who was she? He would be forever in her debt, for he finally had the woman he loved in his arms.

CHAPTER THREE

*W*ith her ear pressed against Walter's hard chest, the rapid thump of the man's heart echoed her own. She should release him, but the warmth and comfort of being held once more was too alluring. Neither of them would expire if she held on to Walter for a moment longer. Henrietta's muscles melted as his palm grazed up and down her spine. She had raised two strapping boys on her own, in no need of a man, but she missed the bond of a confidant. George had been her stoutest supporter and never censured her outspoken ways. Her late husband also had a habit of baiting her to go one step beyond her limits. Never once did she regret the leap of faith George pushed her to take. She couldn't remember the last time she had challenged her boundaries.

Leaning back, she stared at Walter's friendly, warm brown eyes. "Thank you."

"Whatever for?"

RACHEL ANN SMITH

"For keeping your promise to George." She took a step back and fiddled with the silver ship that would be added to her bracelet. "How is it you were even acquainted with George?"

Walter stiffened. "Do you remember the year you were to have your coming out, and we sneaked out to feed the ducks, the ones you believed to be starving in the cold in the middle of Hyde park?"

"Of course." Henrietta remembered it as if it were yesterday. George had saved her the trouble of being paraded before the ton by whisking her away and marrying her.

"You told me you would do anything to avoid the marriage mart. That the thought of being paraded about as if you were a horse at Tattersalls made you feel ill."

She had been rather dramatic in her earlier years. "Yes, it was all very daunting until George rescued me."

"Yes—George was there. He overheard our conversation and hunted me down. Claimed you were an angel sent down from heaven to save his soul. Stated quite emphatically that if I cared a whit about you, I would help him ensure you didn't suffer at the claws of the matrons who would surely tear you to shreds." He tucked his hands behind his back and bowed his head. "I was fourteen. But you treated me as if I were still the ten-year-old boy you found lost in the woods. I wanted you to be happy."

The sun was close to disappearing, and a foreboding chill ran down her spine. "What did George ask of you?"

Walter chuckled. "It's getting late. I shall regale you

with the rest of the story another time. Allow me to escort you back to your carriage."

He hadn't avoided her question with a question of his own; however, he once again delayed answering her question. It was unnerving not to have all the facts. Her deceased husband had been a complex man with many secrets. To find out that the man who fathered her children had maintained a friendship with Walter without her knowledge stung. Ire flowed through her veins. Henrietta marched back to George's grave and fell to her knees. Before she spoke, she glanced over her shoulder. Walter remained where she had left him but turned slightly, giving her privacy she needed. She lowered her voice to a whisper. "Husband, you never told me you saw me that day. I believed you had shared everything with me." A tear rolled down her cheek. George's family history was full of mysteries and secrets. He had been descended from a line of sworn Protectors of the Royal Family—PORFs. And now their eldest, Landon was the holder of an ancient rondure that placed him in the position of Head PORF. She closed her eyes and another tear escaped. George would be so proud of Landon.

Head bent, she leaned her forehead against the cold gray stone. "Will I ever discover the full truth? Or will your actions and need for clandestine activity keep me forever guessing?" Wiping the moisture from her cheek with the back of her glove, Henrietta stood, straightened her spine, and turned to place her hand upon Walter's proffered arm. "I shall require a detailed retelling, Walter. I don't want you to leave one piece of information out, regardless of how you believe I might react. Am I clear?"

They made their way through the cemetery. The darkness cast an eerie mist over them.

With the coach in sight, Walter said, "Henrietta. That is all in the past. What good could come of reliving a period that neither of us can change?"

"I want to know what occurred. I suspect whatever it was, it is the reason you refuse to meet my gaze." She stepped up into the carriage and positioned herself in the far corner of the forward-facing seat, giving Walter ample room to join her.

The tip of his booted foot paused on the step, but the rest of him remained out of sight.

"What are you waiting for? Are you going to join me or not?" The corner of her lips curled into a smile at the memory of asking him the same questions years ago, perched on a tree limb.

Entering the coach, Walter took the rear-facing seat and scowled at her. "Woman, I'm no longer a lad of ten."

Pleased Walter had recalled their first happenstance meeting, Henrietta replied, "I might be old but I'm not blind. I can see you are..." As the words slipped from her mouth, she scanned his strained features. "You have matured into a rather fine-looking gentleman."

His pale cheeks flushed pink. "Flattery will not gain you the information you seek." He removed his hat and placed it upon his knee.

Henrietta took in the sight of his disheveled full head of hair and rubbed tips of her fingers against the soft velvet that lined her gloves. What would it be like to run her hand through his locks? Blinking away her wayward thoughts, Henrietta said, "Ah. Yes, how foolish of me to believe a savvy gentleman such as yourself would simply divulge details." Tapping her forefinger against her chin she continued, "Hm. I hear you have declared it was time for your poor dear nephew, Marquess of Darlington, to marry."

Walter's gaze narrowed even further. "Nicholas is eight-and-twenty. It is time."

"Says the man who's in his forties and never married. Why so eager for him to wed and produce an heir?"

"Nicholas has a duty to the title. To the family."

"Have you considered Nicholas may wish to simply follow in his uncle's footsteps and never marry?"

He let out a sigh. "I have heard the lad bandy it about that if marriage wasn't for me, it wasn't for him either. But the title is not a burden I carry."

Henrietta replied, "Burden? Good gracious, it that what you have raised the boy to believe—that the Marquessate of Darlington is naught but an encumbrance?"

"Regardless of your opinions of my child-rearing skills, the fact remains that Nicholas needs to find a suit-able woman to marry."

"What of Nicholas's happiness? What of love?" Titled or not, every man and woman was entitled to a fulfilling marriage, one whereby there was respect and a healthy dose of passion and love.

"If my nephew is as smart as I believe him to be, he'll refrain from experiencing such emotions."

"Ridiculous." Henrietta crossed her arms. Walter needed her help. A match needed making, and no one was better than Henrietta at such a task. Now she could actively participate in the bustle of the season with a clear purpose—helping two lost souls find love. The jolt of excitement of once again being needed exhilarated her. While her sons believed falling in love with their wives had been all their own doing, it had been years of planning, hundreds of comments and references to her two beautiful and bold daughters-in-law that Henrietta had planted, that resulted in the fine unions. None of which would have been possible without the support and assistance of the Network.

The covert organization was comprised of families who had pledged to serve and protect PORFs for as many generations as there had been PORFs. The quickening of her pulse at launching a new scheme had Henrietta straightening. Yes. She'd use her resources to identify the ideal candidate for Nicholas Weathersbee. "If I assist you in finding a match for Nicholas, will you tell me the tale of how you and George became acquainted and how it came about that it was you my beloved husband entrusted to see to my happiness?"

"Are you suggesting I subject Nicholas to one of your schemes?"

"Not one of mine, one of *ours*. If I remember correctly, together we concocted some rather devilishly clever plans."

"We did, didn't we." Walter chuckled.

Her heart fluttered at the gruff sound. Yes. It would be fun to have a co-conspirator once again. "Well. Do you agree to share your secrets once Nicholas is happily engaged and in love?"

"I do." Walter grinned and nodded. "I do indeed."

Henrietta replayed her terms over in her head. It was always concerning when a man as astute as Walter agreed too easily. Either Walter didn't believe his nephew would be happy, or that he would be in love. If the scheme that she was piecing together was successful, both Walter and Nicholas would find themselves leg-shackled to respectable women of the ton that they loved. She just needed to puzzle out who had captured Walter's attention all these years. Knowing Walter, his secret love was close at hand. Within his reach had he simply dared to take the plunge and declare his feelings.

CHAPTER FOUR

*J*umping out of the Hadfield carriage, Walter slapped his hat back atop his head. *What the blazes have I done?* Of all the idiotic decisions he'd made over the years—continuing to care for a woman he couldn't have, loving her from a distance, sneaking about town leaving her trinkets—agreeing to spend hours upon hours in close contact with Henrietta was by far the most fatuous. He stood with his hand out at the ready, steeling himself for the inevitable thrum he always experienced when Henrietta was within inches. His heart flipped in his chest the moment she placed her hand on his arm and squeezed it as she descended. He was in trouble. The twinkle of mischief blazed in her eyes and he wanted to keep that spark alive—even if it meant risking her finding out about his deepest, darkest secret: his continued infatuation for her.

The red front door to the Hadfield townhouse flew

open to reveal a disgruntled Lord Hadfield. "Where the devil have you been?"

Henrietta stiffened. "Landon! That is no way to speak to your mother."

Landon jutted his chin out in Walter's direction. "The inquiry was intended for Lord Weathersbee, Mama, not you." Walter mentally rummaged through his agenda. He didn't recall having made arrangements to meet Landon. Frozen with one foot on the top step, Walter considered the situation. If he was to finally pursue Henrietta, he'd have to build a rapport with her eldest son. Physically, the lad resembled George and had even inherited the terrible lung condition that took George from this earth. However, Landon's temperament was more akin to his mama's—determined and stubborn. Squaring his shoulders, he stepped up to the landing to come face-to-face with the lad.

Henrietta bustled past her son and shimmied out of her cloak, which the butler silently took from her. "Oh. Then you must escort Lord Weathersbee to your study if the two of you must speak. Where is your wife?"

"I believe you will find Bronwyn is in the library."

"Perfect." Henrietta turned to face Walter. "I shall have Morris bring Bertha's documents for you to review. I look forward to hearing your legal opinion on the matter this eve." Practically skipping, Henrietta left him with her agitated son.

The woman had a way of giving him orders that left him wanting more. He tore his gaze away from the sway of her rounded hips and found himself the recipient of one of Landon's rare smiles that revealed his dimple. Never having been privy to the infrequent expression up close, Walter was caught off guard by the charming display. Smiles in general were used to set another at ease or to provide reassurance, yet the sight of the man's dimple set his nerves on edge. Over the years, Walter had watched Landon become the honorable gentleman standing before him. He was also aware that Landon was extremely protective of his mama. He hoped Landon would one day come to trust him like his papa had.

"Lord Weathersbee, shall we adjourn to the study for a drink?"

Walter removed his hat and allowed the inconspicuous butler to take it along with his coat and gloves. George would be so proud of his son's innate ability to quickly surmise another's motives. Landon had inherited his mother's tenacity, but combined with George's wit and patience, the lad had been a formidable barrister and was now undoubtedly the patriarch of the family.

Walter followed Landon through the townhouse, mumbling, "I need more than a bloody drink, but a French brandy will have to do for now."

Entering Landon's study, Walter's nose twitched at the sweet scent of vanilla. It was familiar, yet the Hadfield women favored floral scents; Henrietta violets and Bronwyn daisies. His mind raced, cross-referencing events and memories. Damnation. The faux flower seller. Reflecting upon it, there had been a multitude of clues that should have had him looking closer at the imposter.

The strong whiff of spices with warm undertones

replaced the feminine scent. Walter took the tumbler Landon held out for him. "My thanks." Lifting the glass in the air, Walter said, "Your mother is the reason I was missing from the offices this afternoon." He followed Landon over to the two wingback chairs facing the fire.

"I received word this afternoon of Mama's visit to the office, followed by your rather rushed departure." Landon settled into his chair. He appeared relaxed, but a tenseness remained in his posture. Walter sipped his brandy as he waited for Landon to begin his inquisition. He should have known Landon would have informants keeping him apprised of the activities at Neale and Sons. Walter suspected many of the employees were directly connected to the Network that vowed to serve PORFs, but he hadn't managed to specifically identify which ones.

Half a glass downed, Landon leaned forward to roll his glass between his palms. "I'm curious. Why did you decide to disclose your secret this year?"

Landon's query was a cold bucket of water tossed in his face. George had mentioned files were maintained on individuals of interest. Walter never considered he was one of them. If George had shared with his son that Walter knew the truth about PORFs, why had Landon not approached Walter previously?

"To what secret are you referring?" He leaned back in his chair.

Waving the empty glass up in the air, Landon replied, "Let me ponder for a moment." He pinned Walter with a look that was frighteningly familiar. It was the same one Henrietta used when she was about to reveal something shocking. "There are a number to choose from. However, shall we start with the fact that you are the one responsible for leaving Mama trinkets annually on the anniversary of my papa's death."

How very shrewd of Landon to allude to his knowledge of Walter's multiple secrets. Knowing it best to never answer a barrister's query without posing one of your own, he released the breath he'd held a moment longer than necessary and asked, "How long have you known?" Landon's answer would at least provide him with an indication as to how long he'd been on the man's watch list.

"Not long." Landon peered into his empty glass and then continued, "Mama loves mysteries, and with Christopher's absence, I thought discovering the identity of her annual gift giver would provide her with the ideal investigation to occupy her time. Since you foiled my plans, care to tell me why you have been secretly giving my mama gifts all these years?"

Fascinating. The boy had provided the typical noncommittal answer expected of a lawyer, yet he elaborated without prompting as to his reasoning. It was Walter's turn to stare into his empty glass. *Not long* could mean years, months, or days. Regardless, Landon knew the truth and there was no reason to further delay answering. "My intentions are honorable. I made a promise to your father."

Landon straightened in his seat. "My papa?" Gone was the relaxed, non-threating PORF. Instead, Walter faced the narrowed gaze of a son ready to defend and protect his mama. "I wasn't aware you were even acquainted with Papa."

"Neither was your mother until today." Walter balanced his glass on the arm of the chair. "In one afternoon, your mother has seen to it I'm embroiled in the matter of Lady Bertha's engagement to Lord Otterman, *and* she has decided to take on the task of assisting my nephew in finding the next Marchioness Darlington." His mind still whirled from how quickly Henrietta had managed to entangle him into her schemes.

"Then I shan't worry about Mama. Matchmaking is her favorite pastime." Landon rose and held out a hand for Walter's empty glass. "Another?"

Walter nodded and handed over his glass. It didn't appear Landon had any intention of cutting their meeting short. At least not until the boy had all the answers he wished to obtain. Returning, Landon offered Walter a glass with a healthy portion of brandy. He took the glass and swirled the amber liquid around and around. Landon was a skilled interrogator; he needed a clear head and his wits about him not to disclose any more secrets. Landon was shrewd and extremely patient.

Landon was the first to break the silence. "I agree with Mama. There is something amiss with Lord Otterman's proposal to Lady Bertha." Landon glanced at Walter over the rim of his glass and slowly lowered it. He gave a piercing stare and added, "I'd like to offer you my assistance in the matter. I might have access to information on the man that could assist."

33

Walter returned Landon's steady gaze. The lad was testing him. It was subtle hint to the secret Network. Walter was no fool. He'd promised George to never disclose his knowledge of PORFs or the Network.

When Walter raised his glass to sip on his brandy, Landon chuckled and said, "I'm happy to hear Mama will have another opportunity to play matchmaker. She's still livid over her failure to act fast enough to see to Theo's happiness, and thank goodness I found Bronwyn before Mama could devise one of her schemes for me."

Ha. Walter had overheard Henrietta's plans for Landon years before the lad proposed. She had shared and debated the details with George during one of her visits to the cemetery. Henrietta had carefully evaluated a number of women from various sets before settling upon Bronwyn. Her elaborate arrangements to place Bronwyn right beneath her son's nose had been a point of frustration for Henrietta for years. But unlike in her youth, Henrietta had learned to excel at the long game.

"Nicholas is no fool and will not be tricked into marrying." As the words slipped over his lips, a shudder rolled through him. Walter gave himself a shake. There was nothing to worry about. Nicholas was levelheaded, intelligent, kindhearted, and loyal. Without question, his nephew would choose wisely. It was simply a matter of convincing the lad he should take action.

"Mama will not resort to trickery." The man's rare dimple reappeared. "Her scheme will all hinge upon her claim that it is simply a matter of numbers and being skilled at identifying the perfect candidate."

Walter's chest constricted. "Pray elaborate."

The lad's broad grin was an exact replica of his papa's. Walter had been the recipient of such a look many a time while George was alive. Even after two decades, the mischievous tilt still had the ability to set bells off in Walter's mind.

Landon said, "Mama will parade as many women as possible before Lord Darlington, and all the while she will be waiting for a tell to present itself."

"A tell?" The future Darlington bloodline was at the mercy of some ambiguous observation.

"Aye." Landon lifted his tumbler back to his lips but before he drained its contents, he said, "A signal. Something that might indicate the potential for a love match."

The boy must think him a fool. Shifting in his seat to stare at the dwindling fire, Walter sighed. "Love is more than physical attraction."

"I wholeheartedly agree. Nonetheless, lord help us all, Mama will be determined to locate Darlington's love match."

"Love match." Walter couldn't believe his ears. Finding a love match for Nicholas would be like finding a four-leaf clover in the streets of London. "A luxury titled gentlemen are rarely afforded. If that is Henrietta's plan, it will be a long, trying season." He raised his glass to his lips. The idea that he'd be in close contact with the woman he'd loved for over three decades, instead of admiring her from afar, had him tilting the tumbler until every last drop wet his palate. Yes, it was going to be a very long season indeed.

His host rose and made his way to the dwindling fire. With a well-placed jab, the boy once again stoked the flames back to life. Poker in hand, Landon said, "I disagree. Many of my titled gentlemen friends have found wedded bliss based on love." He leaned the iron rod back against the wall and clasped his hands behind his back, the stance all barristers assumed before cross examination of a witness. Landon asked, "Would a season in my mama's company be such a trial for you?"

Walter would have to watch his speech in Landon's presence lest he give up too many of his secrets. Landon shared George's razor-sharp mind and the ability to phrase queries that would garner him a wealth of information. Walter may not have gained his qualification at the Inns of Court, but he had gained a sound education at Oxford. Combined with years of negotiating contracts and handling Darlington's affairs until he was of age, it had taught Walter silence was the best answer to all queries you wished to avoid.

Landon raised a hand to make a point. "You and Mama have much in common."

"How so?" He wanted to clasp a hand over his mouth. He was supposed to remain silent.

"You both placed the safety and security of the children in your care above all else."

"Raising my nephews and niece was no hardship." His brothers' children had provided Walter with an abundance of joy over the years. He never regretted his decision to become sole guardian and keep them all under one roof.

"I'm certain Mama would make the same claim."

Walter twisted slightly to meet Landon's keen gaze. "Not an assertion. Merely a fact."

"You share with Mama an innate ability to love others to the detriment of your own needs." Landon began to pace in front of the fire. It was obvious Landon was not done quizzing Walter. "It's purported that you were considered quite the catch during your formidable years, yet none of the ladies were able to convince you to offer for their hand. Widows and mistresses were left broken hearted."

Landon paused and swiveled on his heel to glare down at Walter. "Now that both Christopher and I are wed, Mama deserves and has the freedom to seek out her own happiness. To love again. To be with someone worthy of her love and who will appreciate her unique abilities." Landon's gaze held the look of a predator about to bite down on its prey's neck. The lad was building up to his closing statement.

Walter wanted to bolt for the door, but that was no solution; Landon would simply hunt him down. Carefully crafting his response, Walter answered, "I agree your mama ought to live out the rest of her life in happiness. But Henrietta doesn't need a man—never has."

Landon resumed his seat next to Walter and faced the fire. "Aye, the women in my family are self-sufficient. However, they do deserve to be loved and cherished." Landon tilted his head towards Walter. "Having become reacquainted with Mama, do you fancy yourself up for the challenge?"

It was the question Landon had been building up to and the one Walter suspected was coming. "Beg pardon?" Walter's heart stopped.

"Based on my sources and my own observations, you are in love with Mama. I suspect you have been for years." Landon leaned back and crossed his legs at the ankles. "It is time, Lord Weathersbee, for you to decide whether or not to act upon your desires. Or have you already decided? You did reveal yourself today at my papa's grave."

Not exactly by choice, more due to poor planning and an interfering flower girl. Dammit. Landon was correct. It was time he gathered the courage to act upon his feelings for Henrietta. No more excuses. It had dawned upon him the day Christopher had set sail across the pond with his wife that his nephews and niece should soon be happily settled also. It was time to act. He simply hadn't fully formulated his plan, and until he did he'd remain silent on the topic. "What do you know of Lord Otterman?"

"Before I answer, I want your promise Weathersbee —*if* you choose to pursue my mama *and* you succeed, you will see to her happiness until her last breath." Landon wasn't giving Walter his endorsement to pursue his mama; no, the lad was making it clear that should Walter dare to act, he'd best succeed and not hurt his mama in the process.

Walter inwardly sighed. Could he make the same promise a second time? "Aye, you have my word."

The scratch at the door was well timed. Landon

ordered, "Enter." He rose and Walter followed suit. They meandered over to Landon's desk where the butler presented them with salver of three parchment bundles tied with string. "My thanks, Morris. Is this all there is?"

Good gracious. What marriage agreement required three sheaves of paper?

"Nay, my lord. Lord Otterman's solicitors have yet to provide the final marriage agreement. Once they were advised Neale & Sons intended to review prior to Lady Bertha signing, they claimed there were clerical issues to be fixed."

Landon tapped his forefinger over his chin. "How interesting. If they appear, please bring them to us at once."

"Aye, my lord." Morris bowed and left the room.

Grabbing the bundles from his desk, Landon said, "Rather telling, is it not, that Otterman's lawyers are not forthcoming with the agreement."

"Aye. Pray tell, what are those?"

Landon handed him the first bundle. "Information Mama has gathered." The top sheet was marked with the Hadfield seal.

Walter took the second stack Landon held out for him. "And this is from my sources." Walter glanced down and noted the wax seal was of a harped angel surrounded by laurel leaves. It wasn't anyone's crest that he recognized, yet it was vaguely familiar.

Landon placed the last parcel on top of the others. "And this stack is from my dear cousin Theo, Lady Archbroke."

The slight fragrance of vanilla hit him. Lady Arch-broke! Good god. The woman at the cemetery was the wife of the esteemed Lord Archbroke. He tried to reconcile the quiet, reserved green-eyed beauty he'd met at various ton events with the bold, daring woman he'd encountered earlier. Absurd. He must have had too little sleep or too much brandy. He raised the third bundle closer. His sense of smell was impeccable, a hindrance most of the time, but in this instance, there was no doubt. Lady Archbroke was his mystery flower seller. There was only one way to find out what she knew and why she was involved. He took the bundle to the chair near the fire, untied the string, and began to read the missives, all neatly handwritten and signed *Lady A*.

CHAPTER FIVE

*B*ronwyn gripped the back of the settee as Henrietta rubbed small circles over her daughter-in-law's lower back. "Aww. I'm sorry the bub is causing you such pain." It had been over three decades since she last experienced the effects of pregnancy, but Henrietta remembered them vividly. Her own body was currently undergoing another change. Back aches, knee pain, irregular cycles, and sudden changes in body temperature; all signs Henrietta was no longer in her prime. A pang of loneliness stabbed at her chest. Until her earlier encounter with Walter, forgoing the touch of another had been no hardship. Henrietta spent her energy and time on seeing to the happiness of her two boys and she had been content.

Releasing a long, slow breath, Bronwyn said, "It's not the baby. It's your son who is causing my distress." Glancing over her shoulder at Henrietta, she added, "His constant hovering is not good for my constitution."

Henrietta's heart burst with joy. Landon's actions reinforced how much he cared for his wife. George had mastered the art of showering her with love while simultaneously not restricting her independence. Landon would have to strive to achieve the same. "I shall have a talk with him."

"Would you? That would be grand. He listens to you." Bronwyn rolled her shoulders back and straightened. "Now, how can I assist you?"

For the majority of her life, she'd had only herself to oversee her schemes. Now, she had the unwavering loyalty of her niece Theo and two daughters-in-law to aid her. The girls didn't completely fill the void left by George, but they were boon cohorts.

Henrietta beamed at her daughter-in-law. Years of patience and steering Landon in Bronwyn's direction had proven she was a skilled matchmaker. However, with Walter's rushed timeline to see that his nephew married by the end of the season, Henrietta needed all the assistance she could muster to find a woman for Nicholas. "What do you know of Lord Darlington?"

"Hmm..." Bronwyn pressed her palms to the small of her back, which arched as she raised her chin to the ceiling. "I can request the Network's file on the man. However, it may not contain much." Turning to face Henrietta, Bronwyn's lips formed a lopsided smile. "From my foggy memory, I do recall a notation that the man is the male version of what the ton might call a wallflower. Present at all the functions but prefers to remain on the outskirts."

Henrietta nodded, masking a grin at the Network's observation. "From the few encounters I've had with the boy, I would agree. While he is of sound mind, Nicholas is not particularly striking in looks nor does he wield the charm of a rake."

"Mayhap it is all matter of perspective. Some may even consider classically handsome men rather boring." Bronwyn paced about the drawing room. Like Henrietta, her mind worked best while on the move.

"My dear you are quite right. Nicholas may appear unassuming to us, but I'm certain there is a lady among us who sees what no other can." She believed the statement right down to her feet, which were beginning to ache after a long day of errands. Henrietta rounded the settee and settled upon the soft velvet cushions. "Are you acquainted with anyone you would consider worthy to be the next Marchioness of Darlington?"

"Not at this time." Bronwyn continued to wear a path in the rug. "Cousin Theo will no doubt have a list of eligible young ladies."

"Theo! She is mere weeks away from giving birth. Archbroke should have ensured she was safely ensconced in the country and ready to begin her lying-in months ago." Henrietta's opinions on her niece's decision to stay in town had volleyed over the months. She fully understood her niece's wish to be with her husband; after all Henrietta hadn't spent a single night away from George starting from the day they married until his early departure from this world. However, she hadn't been married to the Secretary of the Home

Office who for certain had an undisclosed number of enemies.

"Mama, you know Theo will not leave his side, and he's currently dealing with the political impact of the king's impending demise. The doctors don't foresee the king to be with us for much longer. Mayhap six months, a year at most."

Henrietta's shoulders rolled slightly forward. "At least Theo has kept her word and refrained from partaking in missions." The Neale blood ran strong in her niece. A will strong enough to challenge societal norms, intelligence to manage a genius, and the physical prowess to launch daggers with deathly accuracy.

"Hmm. I don't believe it. I'm certain she is not lying about as she has everyone convinced... but it won't be me informing her husband of that fact." Bronwyn flopped onto the settee next to Henrietta and stuffed a pillow behind her back.

It wouldn't be surprising if Bronwyn was correct. "What have you heard?"

No one had entered the library, yet Bronwyn still scanned the room. Lowering her voice to a whisper she said, "With the amount of correspondence Cousin Theo is sending, she is single handedly keeping the paper industry in business." Her gaze flickered to the door and then back to Henrietta. "She's also been caught a time or two sneaking out once Archbroke is firmly ensconced at the Home Office."

"We shall have to pay a surprise visit to Theo tomorrow." Henrietta studied her daughter-in-law. A match to a lady of the ton was one thing, but the Network was another pool of women Henrietta wished to consider. "Perhaps you know of someone suitable for Lord Darlington that he might not otherwise be privy to."

Bronwyn's eyes widened in understanding. "I shall carry out the research myself. Do you consider Lord Darlington trustworthy?"

"If he is anything like his uncle Lord Weathersbee, who has proven capable of keeping secrets for decades, he will do." At the mention of Walter, her stomach did a little flip. She'd missed the exhilarating sensation. Walter's intense regard and caring actions prodded Henrietta to acknowledge the fact that her life was not over yet. Her life might no longer center around her boys, but she could still help others. Marrying a PORF had given her life a new purpose and soothed the sting of being disowned. Mayhap Walter had provided her the answer to her fears of what was to come next in her life—assisting others in finding love.

Rolling forward to clasp Henrietta's hand, Bronwyn said, "Perhaps we should conduct our own investigations."

"Brilliant. We shall begin tonight at the Redburns' ball." She squeezed Bronwyn's hand.

Her brow furrowed at her daughter-in-law's deep sigh. "I had hoped to stay in tonight." Bronwyn leaned back and rubbed her slightly protruding stomach.

She hated the idea of Bronwyn in distress. "Very

well, I shall request that Landon escort me, which will give you a few hours' reprieve from my son and provide you an opportunity to reach out to the Network."

Bronwyn beamed. "You truly are the best! A nice long soak in the tub will be heaven."

CHAPTER SIX

*R*esting her gloved hand on her son's arm, Henrietta inhaled deeply as the Redburn butler announced their arrival. "The Earl of Hadfield and Lady Henrietta Neale."

She cringed at the honorific that the ton had automatically adopted upon her return to the social whirl. Years ago, she had opted to be addressed as Mrs. Neale rather than retain the title of lady upon marrying George, which was her right in marrying a younger son of an earl. It had been her way of solidifying in her mind that she was no longer the acknowledged daughter of a duke. But upon Landon's ascent to earl, the ton had ignored her preference. She was reintroduced and announced with the honorific she was born into. Even though two years had passed, Henrietta's skin still crawled at the title of *lady*. A reminder of the family that continued to ignore her very existence. Landon patted her hand and began moving forward, thrusting them into the fray of guests. Every year the number of patrons partaking in the social circuit appeared to increase in size while the number of her acquaintances dwindled.

Landon scanned the crowd. The extra two inches of height he inherited from Henrietta's father was advantageous at events like the Redburn ball. "Weathersbee and Darlington are at the far end of the ballroom, to your right."

She followed his lead as they shifted direction. Their progress was slow, edging their way through the throng of gentlemen and ladies. The orchestra began tuning their instruments for the night's entertainment. Henrietta tapped Landon's arm to gain his attention over the din. "Have you located Lady Bertha?"

His arm shifted beneath her hand as he raised ever so slightly onto the balls of his feet. "Aye. She is retreating to one of the waiting rooms, I believe."

They made another inch or two of progress before coming to a halt. She smiled at the young fresh-faced debutantes making their first appearances in front of them, and through gritted teeth she asked, "And Lord Otterman?"

Landon shook his head. "No sign of the man. He might be hiding in either the billiard room or one of the card rooms."

The squawking of instruments ceased, and guests moved into position on the dance floor. Able to move forward once again, Landon seized the advantage and no longer took mincing steps. "Not to worry, Mama, Weathersbee was rather thorough in his assessment of the documentation you provided."

Henrietta tugged on her son's arm, halting their progress, "What think you of his nephew, Lord Darlington?"

Frowning down at her, Landon said, "I gave you my word to assist with Lady Bertha's representation as Papa would have wished. I shall not involve myself with the matter of Lord Darlington's marital status. I'll leave that matter in your capable hands."

She was in no mood for her son's carefully crafted responses. "I merely need to know—in your opinion, is he a pigeon or not?"

"Most definitely not. Raised by Weathersbee, he is far from an easy mark." The music elevated to a crescendo, and Landon raised his voice slightly to be heard. "If he is anything like his uncle, matrimony will only hold Darlington's interest if the lady can capture his heart."

With a curt nod, she said, "And that is how it should be. With the number of eligible ladies in our favor this season, I'm certain we shall succeed."

"We?"

"Aye. We." She smiled up at her son who had never once let her down. Taking advantage of the thinned crowd, she swiveled and changed their course. "I wish to ensure Lady Bertha is well situated before we make Darlington's acquaintance."

Landon arched a brow, which Henrietta ignored as she moved in the direction of one of the smaller parlors.

Crossing the threshold, she spied a number of familiar matrons, chaperones, and spinsters gathered in the parlor. Henrietta's spine stiffened. The horrid Lord Otterman was the center of attention seated next to Bertha. The cad's feigned adoration had Henrietta moving faster, nearly dragging Landon by the hand like she had when he was a boy.

Lord Otterman was a fake. It was the man's body language that gave him away. Never leaning in towards Bertha. Always away. He maintained the socially acceptable distance constantly like a shield. Not once had Henrietta spied a conspiratorial glance or a spark of desire in the man for her friend. Lord Otterman might have convinced the masses he was in love, but Henrietta knew the truth. The man was using her friend, but for what purpose she had yet to discover.

Quickly assessing how to best extricate Bertha away from the blackguard, Henrietta whispered, "Landon, ask Lady Bertha to dance. Find out what you can."

With the last strains of the country reel concluding, Landon dutifully and without question made an elegant bow before her friend. "Lady Bertha, would you care to dance?"

A pretty flush rose to Bertha's cheeks as she placed her hand into Landon's outstretched one. "Lord Hadfield, it would be an honor." Henrietta admitted she herself would have blushed if a handsome young man asked her to dance. An image of Walter flashed before her. She tucked the secret wish that Walter would ask her to dance away and watched Landon lead Bertha onto the dance floor.

Henrietta's skin pebbled as the temperature within the room fell a few degrees. She glanced at the guests closest to her. She was the recipient of more than one glacial look.

Lord Otterman stood glaring at her and leaned forward to growl, "You will not succeed in breaking off our engagement. Meddle in someone else's affairs." Turning on his heel, he left the room. Instead of heading towards the dance floor as Henrietta had expected, he rotated and headed in the opposite direction, only confirming in Henrietta's mind the man held no real tendre for Bertha.

"Really, Hen." Lady Beatrice, Bertha's younger spinster sister pouted.

Henrietta took the spot on the settee Bertha had vacated. She was about to reply when Beatrice let out a sigh. "Why did you have to go and chase Otterman away?" Dreamy-eyed Beatrice continued, "He's so in love with Bertha. He can't stand to be in a room without her."

Lady Marion seated in the chair nearest to them asked, "Why must you keep interfering?"

Henrietta twisted at the waist to face Lady Marion. Her old nemesis was still the image of perfection. Not a strand of hair out of place. Her coiffure beautifully created with just enough face paint to cover the fine lines that came along with age. The woman always left Henrietta tongue tied, giving Lady Marion the opportunity to add,

"You were a meddlesome harpy before you were disowned, and nothing has changed. You should be ashamed, attempting to destroy Bertha's chance at happiness."

The accusation stabbed Henrietta in the heart. Lady Marion had never liked her, but when no one spoke up in her defense, she understood she was no longer welcome amongst the small group of women she once considered friends. Calmly raising to her feet, she did not dare speak in case her voice cracked. Instead she gave Beatrice a curt smile and fled the room, headed towards the terrace. She would not let Lady Marion or the others see the dampness swelling in her eyes. No. She'd rather be roasted on a spit than let that lot see her cry.

She skirted the masses, keeping her gaze lowered and staying close to the outer wall. She was about to slip through the terrace doors when a hand at her elbow stalled her progress.

"Henrietta, what is the matter?" She turned at the warm familiar voice. Walter.

Her breath caught at the sight of him in his sophisticated evening attire. His stark white cravat elegantly knotted. The light gray-blue waist coat almost shimmered in the candlelight. Ruffled sleeves peeked out from his solid black jacket. She glanced up and found Walter examining her ensemble with the same intensity she'd seen in his gaze earlier at the cemetery. The urge to wrap her arms about him and share her troubles like she had when they were children had her almost taking a half step closer to the man.

Instead, she plastered a smile and presented her hand

to the young man standing wide eyed next to Walter. "Lord Darlington, it is a pleasure to meet you."

As courtesy dictated, he took her hand and politely bowed. "The pleasure is all mine, Lady Henrietta. My uncle has spoken highly of you." He released her hand and edged an inch closer to his uncle.

"Oh, dear me. The stories you must have heard." Henrietta teasingly winked and waited for his reaction.

The twitch at the corner of Lord Darlington's lip proved the boy had a sense of humor. She assessed him from head to toe, and when Darlington's cheeks flushed a deep red, Bronwyn's words from earlier rang true. Henrietta would wager her entire monthly pin money that the boy was still a virgin. She snuck a glance at Walter, engaged in a side conversation with another guest. She wondered if Walter was aware his nephew at the age of eight-and-twenty remained an innocent.

Henrietta surmised finding the perfect bride for Walter's nephew was going to be a challenge. If her instincts were correct, it wasn't being leg shackled that the boy resisted, it was the marriage bed he feared. Darlington possessed the same confident yet innocent gaze as George had when they had said their vows. Knowing of George's fears, Henrietta was sympathetic to Darlington's plight. It reinforced her desire to find him a love match. But in order to succeed, she needed to know more about the man. "Lord Darlington, I would be in your debt if you wouldn't mind taking this old woman out onto the dance floor."

Henrietta's bold request startled Walter into a half-turn, revealing her son. What the blazes was Landon discussing in hushed tones with Walter?

Darlington distracted her with a pleasant smile. "It would be my honor to dance with you this eve." He offered Henrietta his arm, and she was pleasantly surprised to feel lean, hard muscles under his jacket. If one looked closely, Darlington was definitely no wall-flower. She was on the hunt for a lady who would dare Darlington to shed his shy exterior. The dance floor was an ideal location to start assessing candidates.

Henrietta lengthened her stride to keep up with the young man. "Your uncle has recruited me to find you a lady this season."

Darlington slowed his pace and with a slight nod said, "Aye. He informed me of your arrangement." The boy didn't object to her involvement, he merely sounded resolved. He was either a very trusting soul or he respected his uncle's decisions. Her son would not have been as accommodating as Darlington had he known her involvement in ensuring he was happily wed.

She caught sight of Landon moving through the crowd towards the billiards room. Walter was not beside Landon, nor was he close by. Walter had somehow again faded into the shadows. They continued to weave through the crowd. The closer they got to the dance floor, the more rigid Darlington's movement became. Henrietta nervously glanced at the boy. After they had been married but a week, George proclaimed martial relations emulated the act of dancing with the ideal partner. He claimed it wasn't so much as knowing the correct steps but who you partnered with. She gave Darlington's arm a squeeze. "Would you care to share with me your preferences in a lady?"

Halting mid-step, Nicholas frowned and said, "Aside from having the necessary skills to run a household, I don't believe I have any."

"None at all?" She needed to ferret out information from the boy. A reel upon the dance floor would not allow her to gain the details required to find him a suitable wife. "Perhaps a stroll about the room would be best."

Darlington's muscles relaxed beneath her fingers. With a nod, he switched directions, and they began to make a circuit about the room. Darlington tugged at his cravat and asked, "Is it ignorant of me to believe I shall simply know when I meet the right woman?"

"Hmm. Ignorant? Definitely not, although some might call it idealistic." Drumming her fingers in time with the music upon his arm, Henrietta continued, "However, if you continue to opt to stand against the wall at such events as this, instead of asking any of the delightful women present to dance, how will you ever find a woman to love?"

A crinkle formed in the center of his youthful forehead. "You believe dancing is the key."

"Aye. You're searching for the woman who feels right in your arms. A partner who moves with you in anticipation of your next step. The lady who you dare to take that extra half inch to be closer to. That is the lucky woman who should be the next Marchioness of Darlington."

Since her reentrance into society, Henrietta had declined a number of offers to dance, opting to dance only with her sons at balls. Tonight, her imagination supplied the image of herself being twirled about by a gentleman—not any gentleman; no, it was Walter's strong arms that she was fantasizing about.

"My uncle mentioned you didn't mince words." Nicholas glanced about the room and sighed. "I suppose then I shall need your assistance in guiding me as to whose dance card I should be seeking to fill."

"We shall survey your options as we make our round." Henrietta gave him a broad smile, and she was pleasantly surprised to see the corner of Nicholas's lips curve. "We will need to find a lady who can make you smile, for you are rather handsome when you do."

They resumed their stroll about the room. "Then we are on the hunt for a woman much like yourself."

Henrietta snorted. "Oh, dear, now you have given me an impossible task."

He's frown reappeared. "Surely not impossible. But I believe I would prefer a woman who voiced her thoughts and opinions. A lady's mind is quite confounding."

Among the crowd, a familiar young face caught Henrietta's attention. Lady Bertha's paid companion, Miss Marina White. The girl was Bertha's distant cousin or niece. Narrowing her gaze, Henrietta focused her attention upon the girl. Miss White was quiet but quick as a whip. However, the girl took great lengths to avoid the company of men. Knowing the males in her family, it wasn't a shock. Henrietta set herself the goal to find out if

Miss White possessed the qualities Darlington was looking for. She contemplated Bertha's description of the girl—pleasant and sensible. Neither particularly met Darlington's wishes. However, her intuition told her Miss White was worth investigating.

Conceiving a plan to get the two together, Henrietta raised her gloved hand to her cheek and said, "Oh, dear."

Darlington slowed his steps and asked, "Whatever is the matter?"

Turning in Marina's direction, Henrietta said, "My dear friend's companion is being shuffled about by the crowd and towards the terrace doors no less. She could easily be dragged out into the gardens. We must rescue her." Quickening her pace so Nicholas had no choice but to follow, Henrietta headed straight toward the girl.

As they approached, Miss White's pleasant smile gave way to a fierce scowl.

Nicholas blurted, "You. What are you doing here?"

Henrietta swatted the boy's arm and reached out to grasp the young woman's hand before she could flee. "Miss White. You mustn't stand so close to the terrace doors. Goodness knows what could happen to you."

"My thanks for your concern, my lady; however, I'm quite capable of defending myself. Aren't I, Lord Darlington?"

Before the boy could answer, Henrietta stated, "Well, it is clear the two of you are already acquainted." How interesting. Henrietta had never witnessed this side of Miss White's personality.

In unison, the pair answered, "Unfortunately."

Ah. They thought alike. That was a good sign. But the darts they were throwing at each other with their gazes was not. Turning towards Miss Marina White, Henrietta said, "Pray tell, how is it you know each other?"

Miss White's lips thinned, and it was Darlington who answered. "I received a missive from my uncle this afternoon requesting I pay a visit to Lady Bertha's residence to obtain a copy of the marriage settlements. Miss White mistook me for an intruder."

"Is that true?" Henrietta asked.

Marina bobbed her head once and said, "Aye, my lady. In my defense, Lord Darlington was hardly forthcoming with an explanation for his visit. I found him loitering in the foyer peering into the study." Miss White's eyes flickered over at Darlington before she added, "The questionable motives of the men in our family have instilled in me to use caution at all times."

"I see." Henrietta paused and assessed Darlington's defensive posture and then turned slightly to view Miss White. The girl's straight spine and rolled back shoulders told Henrietta she wasn't about to let Darlington have the last word. While the pair were engaged in a silent standoff, Henrietta was mentally deciding upon her next move —she needed a reason for the young couple to be in each other's company, and often. Mayhap Walter could assist with providing Darlington's schedule.

Breaking eye contact, Nicholas clasped his hands behind his back and turned to face Henrietta. "My lady, might I suggest we continue our route? It is clear Miss White is in no need of rescuing."

Henrietta tugged Marina in front of her and within inches of Darlington. "I think not. I suggest instead you do the gentlemanly thing and ask Miss White to dance."

Again in unison, the pair uttered in shock, "Beg pardon?"

Henrietta smiled in triumph and then jumped at Walter's gruff voice behind her. "What a grand idea. Nicholas, you are safe. I'm certain Miss White shall refrain from inflicting any bodily harm upon you whilst on the dance floor."

Where the devil had Walter come from? Engrossed in her matchmaking scheme, she'd let her guard down. Anger at her own folly rolled through her and heated her cheeks. Knowing her surroundings at all times was a skill she had mastered as a PORF decades ago. Normally her anger dissipated quickly, but she continued to experience the wave of fire that warmed her blood. She glanced about their small group and noted Walter had claimed the spot directly to her left. They had never been this close in a public setting, which set Henrietta's mind to wondering why.

Walter gave his nephew a pointed look. Darlington expelled a breath and executed an elegant bow. "Miss White, would you care to dance?"

A mischievous glint appeared in the girl's eyes. "Lord Darlington, I believe I would." As Miss Marina White placed her hand in Darlington's, Henrietta noted the slight jolt of awareness in the young couple's eyes. She continued to watch the pair join the line of dancers.

Henrietta giggled. "I'm glad to see Nicholas had the

sense to wear Hessians this eve, or he might not survive Miss White's attentions."

"She is a clever chit." Walter chuckled. "You're not considering her as a potential match for Nicholas are you?"

She turned to face Walter. Her shoulder brushed against his solid chest. Her cheek burned once again at the memory of having been pressed up against the man. Flustered she replied, "I believe Miss White an excellent candidate."

His head angled inquisitively. "How did you come to that conclusion? The pair can scarcely bear each other's company. Hardly what I'd deem a love match."

"Love presents itself in a variety of ways and often in the moments you least expect." Henrietta pondered over her retort.

She swayed slightly closer to the man who had held her securely in his arms. The craving to be held once more startled Henrietta, who had reconciled herself to the fact she'd already been fortunate to have the love of a man. To seek out love a second time would be foolish. Yet Walter's close proximity and his effect upon her challenged her presumptions. She placed her hand on the base of her throat. "I'm a tad parched. Will you please escort me to the refreshments table?"

"What an excellent idea, my dear." Oblivious to his impact upon her, Walter presented his arm. "I was wise to seek out your assistance. We can venture closer to Nicholas and ensure Miss White has indeed refrained from harming the boy." He smiled down at her. "You are magnificent."

Henrietta linked her arm through his and walked in silence next to a version of Walter that had her at sixes and sevens. She'd had the good fortune of a loving husband and the love of two sons. Yet Walter's praise and adoring looks filled a void in her heart that she hadn't known existed.

WALTER REVELED in the warmth seeping through his jacket from Henrietta's gloved hand upon his arm. For two years he had debated how to best approach Henrietta without making a fool of himself. A small shove from an interfering PORF dressed as a flower seller set off a cascade of events that on their own were innocuous but cumulatively had Walter's heart and mind in knots. He lifted his gaze to the captivating woman next to him. She was as beautiful today as she had been when he first fell in love with her three decades before. The years had been kind to them both, and with his niece having reached majority, he legally was no longer bound to be a guardian. Filling his days at Neale & Sons had been the first step to reentering Henrietta's world. When Henrietta's beguiling smile and the mischievous twinkle in her eyes were trained on him, the rest of the world ceased to exist. The exhilaration of being in her company was addictive.

Making little progress through the crowded ballroom,

Walter sighed. "I'm sorry to inform you, but it appears you are not the only lady in need of refreshment."

"I can't see a blasted thing." Henrietta rose onto her tiptoes.

"Might I suggest an alternative." He waited for her to face him and then summoned the courage to pose the question he'd asked a million times in his mind. "Dear Henrietta, would you care to dance with me?" The air in his lungs burned as he waited for her answer. Since her return to society, she had refused every other gentlemanly offer, preferring to remain steadfast in the matrons' drawing room.

Henrietta's eyes widened. "You want to dance with me?"

"I don't see another Henrietta about, do you?" He looked to his left then right.

Bobbing a quick curtsy, she answered, "It would be an honor to partner with you this eve." Her pretty, rounded cheeks were flushed with color.

As they made their way through the wave of guests exiting the dance floor, a barrage of elation, terror and triumph rolled through Walter. Henrietta squeezed his arm and gave him a reassuring smile, which calmed his nerves for a moment before he realized he'd lost track of the program for the evening. What was to come next—the cotillion? A quadrille? His heart raced as couples next to them took their position. It was to be a waltz! At the prospect of whirling Henrietta about for thirty minutes, in what some still considered a scandalous display, his pulse accelerated and his muscles tensed. The pace at which he was becoming reacquainted with Henrietta was dizzying, yet he'd not forgo the opportunity after fantasizing about the woman for the majority of his life.

Glancing about the room he became aware of the covert glances and the unfurling of fans by many of their acquaintances standing nearby. Walter frowned, noting the evil glares shot in Henrietta's direction especially from a gaggle of women huddled at the end of the refreshments table.

"Ignore them—they are merely jealous." Henrietta's smile remained but her voice held an edge that had not existed earlier.

He settled one hand at the center of her back and tightly clasped her hand in the other. "Jealous?"

"Aye, it is rumored you rarely dance." There was a sing-song lilt to her statement, which meant only one thing—she was leaving out pertinent details.

He braced himself for her answer and said, "And?"

"And... it has been noted over the years, you only subject yourself to the exercise with widows... widows who hoped to have you warm their beds. However, you fulfilled the wishes of a select few and for short periods at a time." She winked at him, settling her hand upon his shoulder. "I can see you are shocked by the news. Yet even as a boy you held a certain allure."

Said the woman who crushed his heart at the age of fourteen. Humph. A much younger version of himself flashed before him, kneeling, holding Henrietta's hand, and declaring his intention to marry her one day. While she'd claimed she cared nothing for the ramifications of marrying a man four years her junior, she would not have him ostracized from the ton due to her unconventional ways. Believing he would fail to change Henrietta's stubborn mind, the younger and less experienced version of himself caved to her insistence on remaining friends. Knowing of her wish to marry for love, he had convinced himself that she wouldn't find another that would love her as much as he. That he had time. Except he had not envisioned the existence of a kind, generous, honorable soul like George Neale.

The music began and he set them into motion. Henrietta was light on her feet, and as the seconds passed, his muscles began to relax as they moved as one. Confident he'd not step on her toes, Walter asked, "Did the gossip regarding my choice of partners influence your decision to accept my offer to dance?"

Her steps faltered slightly but he caught her and twirled her until her smile returned. "I'm a realist, Walter. I'm fully aware that I hurt you, deeply, the night I declined the chance of having you as a husband. I have not forgiven myself for causing you pain, nor do I expect your forgiveness."

He leaned in and said, "I forgave you long ago, my dear. Long ago."

She tilted her head and pinned him with a curious stare. "Does that mean you..." He switched directions to avoid a couple whizzing by. Regaining her balance, she continued, "Are the rumors true? Do you only dance with those you wish to bed?"

He raised an eyebrow and the pinkish tinge in her

cheeks deepened. Since her return to society, he had fantasized on numerous occasions of boldly approaching and whisking her away from balls, soirees, the theatre. But his fantasies always abruptly ended when reality set in. He couldn't steal her away, and he certainly couldn't sneak her into his nephew's townhome with his niece in residence. Tonight was no different. He cleared his throat.

"You know as well as I the dangers of believing gossip."

She edged closer, the scent of violets tickling his nose. "My thanks for not answering a question with a question. However, your reply still has me curious." Henrietta wagged her brows at him like she had when they were children, but they were no longer in their youth and her actions caused more than his heart to leap. He needed a distraction, or with their close proximity, Henrietta would soon find out that the rumors were indeed true. In his peripheral vision, he caught sight of his nephew standing alone. "It appears Miss White has had enough of Nicholas. She has abandoned him."

He led her into a turn so she could witness the dark scowl that masked his nephew's fine features. She followed his lead with ease, her body moving in time with his. Before his mind could ponder over their compatibility in bed, he asked, "Do you know how old Miss Marina White is? I don't recall which year she made her debut."

Squinting up at him, Henrietta said, "I believe Miss White shall soon turn nine-and-twenty."

He shortened his step to avoid yet another errant couple. "How interesting that you would endorse Nicholas marrying an older woman."

"Older?" The surprise in her voice sent another jolt of pleasure through him. It was a rare occasion for the woman to be caught unawares.

"Aye, Nicholas has only recently turned eight-and-twenty himself."

"That would make Miss White his senior by mere months. If it is true your nephew is wise beyond his years, her age should not prove to be an issue."

The crinkle in her brow and the slight waver in her normally steady tone raised Walter's suspicions. "Nevertheless, she is older and no doubt it would be commented upon." The views and the opinions of the ton remained stilted regarding unions between an older woman and a gentleman. From the deepening of her frown, it was apparent Henrietta remained unconvinced the benefits of such a union would outweigh the censure of the ton regardless if the couple were in love. However, he hoped if Miss White were to capture Nicholas's heart, his nephew would be bold and brave enough to offer for the woman's hand.

Henrietta tilted her head slightly. He followed the direction of her gaze that was sadly no longer focused upon him. Landon glared back at him. If Henrietta was correct that it was common knowledge that he only danced with those he let into his bed, surely her son had also heard the same. Walter grumbled, "I believe your son is unhappy with the sight of you in my arms."

"Will Landon's displeasure prevent you from asking me to dance in the future?" Henrietta's lips twitched at the corners.

He could not stop his own grin from appearing as he replied, "Nay. I shall not be thwarted. Will you be discouraged from accepting?"

"Landon is well aware that I do as I please." Her gaze shifted to their right. "It appears your nephew hasn't entirely given up his pursuit of Miss White."

Walter scanned the far wall and caught Nicholas granting a rather perturbed Miss White a rare but charming lopsided grin. How peculiar for Nicholas to be revealing a side of himself that was typically reserved only for family. Rather than being charmed, Miss White jutted her nose up in the air and stomped on his poor nephew's booted toe as she turned and left Nicholas's side.

Henrietta laughed. "Mayhap I should stop allowing you to distract me and *we* should consider searching for other eligible ladies."

Walter let out a half sigh, half chuckle. "That may well be a wise option."

Dread seeped into his bones as the last notes of the waltz were played. "I suppose it would be scandalous for us to continue our investigations here on the dance floor."

"Why, Walter Weathersbee, you surprise me. To actually think I used my pin money as a girl to bribe you to engage in dance practice with me."

A full hearty laugh escaped him. It was good to share the fonder moments of their childhood. "You never benefited from the blunt you invested in me. However, you shan't tonight either. Landon shall descend upon us shortly."

Henrietta spun out of his arms and faced her son. "Ah, my dear boy. Have you come bearing news?"

Landon arched one eyebrow in his mother's direction. "I have indeed received word from my runners. However, now is not the time nor the location for such discussion. Might I suggest we retire for the evening?" The boy nodded, finally acknowledging Walter. "Lord Weathersbee, if you and your nephew are not otherwise engaged later this eve, perhaps you will join me for a drink at my club?" Landon pulled out his pocket watch. "Say, on the hour?"

Walter was no fool. Landon had issued the order in the disguise of a friendly invitation for the benefit of those within hearing. Nicholas and he would be expected to appear at Brooks, and from Landon's tone the news he was about to receive was not of the good sort. Walter nodded. "I shall extract my nephew from the fray." Turning to Henrietta, he said, "My thanks for a very enlightening evening. It shall be a rather interesting season if tonight was an indication as to what is to come."

Landon whisked his mother away, and instead of feeling regret as he usually did at seeing Henrietta leave, hope flourished. It may have taken him over three decades to emerge from the shadows, but now that he had, there was no going back.

CHAPTER SEVEN

*N*icholas hobbled next to Walter as they were escorted to a section of Brooks neither of them had access to previously. The footman halted and opened a door to a dimly lit private parlor. The clandestine location, the sparse but luxurious furnishings inside reminded Walter he was dealing with the Head PORF, privy to information and resources that most were unaware even existed. Walter stripped out of his great coat, handed his hat, coat and gloves to the stoic footman, and waited for Nicholas to do the same. Hands clasped behind his back, he entered the room, noting the faint scent of sandalwood and the distinct lack of cigar and tobacco smoke. Landon's lung condition made him hypersensitive to air particulates, just like his papa.

To his left, Nicholas fell into one of the leather chairs facing the fire. His nephew stretched out his leg and rolled his foot at the ankle. "The cursed woman stomped on my toes."

Opting to stand when Landon arrived, Walter made his way to the mantel to face both the door and Nicholas. "What did you do or not do that prompted the sweet Miss White to act in such a manner?"

"Sweet! That woman is all vinegar—a complete harridan." Nicholas huffed and crossed his arms over his chest.

Walter studied his nephew's perturbed features. Nicholas rarely let his emotions rule his behavior, and if this was the effect Miss White had on his nephew, he hoped Henrietta would quickly identify other potential ladies. Henrietta. Would he ever not feel the pangs of parental guilt? Probably not. While he had been experiencing the best eve in the company of the woman he loved, his poor nephew had been put through the wringer. "She's a harridan, is she? I hope you refrained from referring to her as such."

"Of course I abstained from using such language in the presence of a lady." Nicholas heaved in a deep breath. "Miss White lured me into believing she could be pleasant company while we danced. No discussion of the weather or other such nonsense. She even smiled a time or two, but she fled as soon as the last note was played. Hoping to become better acquainted with the version of the lady I danced with, I sought out Miss White." The lad let out deep sigh that Walter knew all too well. It meant Nicholas was about to make some type of confession. "I made a remark that her position as companion was in jeopardy now that her cousin intended to marry Lord Otterman." His nephew shook his head woefully from side to side. "Miss White proceeded to accuse me of calling her long in the tooth, an aging spinster with no prospects, amongst other less polite phrases, and proceeded to punctuate her statements by stomping on my toes as she left my company."

Nicholas was not one to mince words—a trait that many did not admire or understand. "The female brain is complex, my dear boy. In my experience, those of fairer sex often interpose random suppositions at a mere blink of an eye or the twitch of a brow. Confounding, to be certain."

"More like mystifying." Nicholas crossed his feet at the ankles and leaned back to stare up at the ceiling. "How am I ever to find a lady to wed?"

A deep chuckle echoed through the room. Landon's tall form entered, and he sauntered over to the chair next to Nicholas. "You shall have to dance with every eligible lady this season. The lady you are most compatible with on the dance floor will also prove to be a fine bed partner. Thus ensuring you see to your duty that the next heir to the Darlington title is sired."

Nicholas straightened and faced Landon. "Your mama shared the same theorem with me earlier; however, not verbatim."

What an interesting hypothesis. Walter recalled Henrietta's adorably flushed cheeks as he pulled her closer, moving in unison with ease across the dance floor. Yes, he could well imagine Henrietta would be a lively bed partner. The woman had danced through his dreams many times over the decades, sometimes naked. But in recent years, she'd appeared more frequently devoid of clothing, riding him hard with her glorious hair falling over plump breasts. The fantasy made it necessary to shift his weight, bringing Landon's attention to fall upon him. The boy's dark scowl reminded him now was not the time nor the place to be picturing Henrietta in bed.

Thankfully Nicholas's "Humph" had Landon returning his attention to Walter's nephew, who inquired, "How many ladies trod upon your poor feet prior to dancing with the Countess of Hadfield?"

Landon revealed that elusive dimple. "Interestingly, I never danced with my dear wife prior to our wedding. However, I can't find fault in my mama's theorem. It was only after a rather poignant discussion with a lady I now deem a dear friend, on the dance floor, that I realized the depths of my love for Bronwyn."

Walter moved to the side bar and poured the dark, rich brandy into a tumbler, taking a moment for himself. His hand shook as he lifted the glass to his lips now that he'd made the decision to pursue his dreams and risk rejection.

Behind him Nicholas groaned. "Perhaps I shall settle for a bluestocking or a wallflower and save my toes."

Walter turned to find Landon consoling Nicholas with a pat on the shoulder. "I wish you well for the season, Darlington. My mama will not be satisfied with a marriage of convenience nor a union based on anything other than love." Landon stood and joined Walter. "It is not your nephew's marital status that I've come to discuss. My informants believe Otterman may be maintaining a family in secret." He held out a parchment for Walter.

Taking the folded piece of paper, Walter scanned the note. "I shall take care of the investigations myself."

"It might be wise to take Darlington with you."

"I think not." Landon was not in charge of him or his nephew. "The slums of St. Giles is no place for Nicholas."

Nicholas stood and puffed out his chest. "Uncle. I promise not to make a hash of it like I did with Miss White. Allow me to accompany you."

His nephew had little reason to venture far from Mayfair. Nicholas was not the type to wench nor wallow in his cups. Time for Walter to stop coddling the boy. "Very well." He gave Landon a nod and began to make his way to the door. "Let's be done with this business."

Knowing Henrietta, she would only be willing to wait until morn before descending upon him for answers. Walter wasn't sure if the tightness in his chest was in anticipation of seeing her early in the morn or due to anxiety of finding out once more that a gentleman of the ton would conduct himself with such dishonor. Leading the way through the halls of Brooks, Walter stopped momentarily to accept the assistance of the footman with his outer garments. At the mention of Miss White's name, Walter slowed his movements and pretended to focus on buttoning his great coat. His hearing wasn't as sharp as it once was, but he could still make out Landon's serious tone. "My advice, Darlington, is to choose with your heart, not your mind. And I wouldn't be so hasty to rule out the lovely Miss Marina White. It was clear the woman has an effect upon you."

Nicholas replied, "Lovely? That is not a descriptor that comes to mind when I think of her."

"Hmm... and what words would you use?" Landon asked.

"Obstinate. Mayhap infuriating." Nicholas released a resigned sigh and added, "But also beautiful. Clever. Worthy of a gentleman who will make her swoon and disabuse her belief that all men prioritize themselves above all else. While I'm certain I'd be perfectly happy in a union with the lady, Miss White made it quite clear this evening that all I am capable of evoking within her are unladylike thoughts and the wish to cause me bodily harm."

Landon's hand landed solidly on Nicholas's shoulder. "Miss White sounds perfect."

Walter agreed.

Stepping out into the muggy night air, he drew Landon aside. "Please advise your mama of Nicholas' preference for Miss White. The boy will need all the support in order to gain the chit's hand."

"Not to worry, Weathersbee. Mama has everything well in hand with regard to the matter of your nephew. She, however, is not happy with our lack of progress regarding Lady Bertha's continued courtship and engagement to Otterman. Mama claims the longer we take to prove that the man is indeed a cad, the more in love Lady Bertha will become, thus the graver the impact once the scandal becomes known by all."

"If Otterman does maintain a separate family, we shall handle the matter. You have your own dealings to worry about—namely seeing to it you survive the birth of your first child."

It wouldn't do to involve Landon. The boy was driven by honor and would embroil himself in a duel if he deemed it necessary. Given the male relations of Lady Bertha and Miss White had been absent and remiss in their duties to care for the women, they would not be likely to risk their heads in a duel to defend either lady's honor. Walter would have to take matters into hand and hope it did not lead to an early morning meeting with Otterman in some damp, godforsaken field.

He placed a foot upon the coach steps to follow Nicholas, but stalled when Landon cleared his throat. "Weathersbee, before you go, there is one more matter I'd like to address."

"Aye." Twisted at the waist, Walter waited for Landon to meet his gaze. "Well, what is it, Hadfield?"

Landon had grown into a man that Walter was certain George would have been extremely proud of. The boy had restored the family coffers upon inheriting the earldom and had fulfilled his duties with grace and honor that most of the gentlemen born first in line lacked. Landon was held in high esteem by his peers. But the man standing before Walter looked as uncertain about what he had to say as Walter must have when he was a lad of fourteen and confessed his love for Henrietta to the man who fathered Landon.

Landon cleared his throat. "Weathersbee, I had my

doubts when Christopher trusted you with our papa's firm, and you have proven my worries on that front were unwarranted. However, it is apparent I was unclear earlier. Mama deserves happiness, not scandal."

"Beg pardon?"

"You. Her. Dancing." Landon tugged on his gloves and flipped up the collar of his great coat. "And I don't care to witness her frowning."

Walter stood frozen as Landon turned and left. What the bloody hell had just happened?

Nicholas poked his head out of the coach door. "Uncle, is something amiss?"

Shaking his head, Walter vaulted up into the coach and settled in next to Nicholas. "Nay, naught is amiss." Unaccustomed to being under such scrutiny, Walter would have to be more mindful that he was once again under the watchful eyes of PORFs and their Network.

CHAPTER EIGHT

*W*alter dipped his chin down to his chest and took in a shallow breath. The faint hint of violets bolstered his spirits before the stench of debris from street markets and refuse marked their entrance into the rookery. The coach continued to jostle them about as the wheels ran over the uneven cobbled streets.

Nicholas planted his hand against the coach wall to steady himself. "We are no longer in Mayfair." His nephew peered out the coach window and the boy's gaze was almost immediately filled with sadness. "The mere thought that a gentleman would even consider setting up a family in such conditions causes my stomach to ache. I hope Hadfield's informants were wrong."

Perhaps sheltering his nephew all these years was not as wise as he once thought. The undermining nattering of family members roared in Walter's ears. He shook his head and pressed himself deeper into the corner of the coach. "As you are keenly aware, life is unpredictable."

Nicholas let the coach curtain fall back into place. "And you taught me it is not the unforeseen events that shape us; it is our choices, how we decide to react, that forms our future. An honorable man would claim his offspring and provide for them, not banish them to live in squalor."

The coach rolled to a stop and the door swung open. Walter shifted forward, slightly hunched over and ready to exit. "Remember, we are here to investigate, not make judgments."

Emerging from the coach, Walter glanced down the alley and spotted a gentleman with his head in his hands sitting upon the third step up, in front of a dwelling with its windows partially boarded up with wood. Walter set off down the path, side-stepping stacks of crates and avoiding eye contact with the scantily clad ladies of the night.

Nicholas was close on his heels. "Is that Otterman?"

They stopped in front of the dilapidated building, and Lord Otterman lifted his head, blinked, then let his head fall back into his hands. "Nick off, Weathersbee. Leave me be."

Walter ignored the man's request. "Good gracious, Otterman, what are you doing loitering out here?"

Lord Otterman shook his head not bothering to look up. "I'm warning you, Weathersbee, dancing with Lady Henrietta is a dangerous affair." He glanced up, revealing bloodshot eyes. "You don't want to attract the attention of her son."

"We are not here to discuss the Hadfields," Walter replied.

"Ah, but it is the Hadfields, that meddling Lady Henrietta, who have brought you here. Now, my failure will be revealed to all and sundry."

Walter crouched down in front of Otterman but recoiled at the smell of gin and ale. "Otterman, focus and answer me—what are you doing here?" Walter motioned to the house in front of him.

"I'm waiting." Lord Otterman swayed a little to his left.

Nicholas stepped forward and braced the man by the shoulder. "Lord Otterman, we don't have all eve and I'm running out of patience. What are you waiting for?"

Turning to look over his shoulder at the door behind him, Lord Otterman said, "She won't answer my letters. She claims I'll be happier without her." Hands clenched at his knees, Otterman continued, "I'm denied the right to see my own damn son. Heir to a destitute and damaged title, but a title nonetheless."

Nicholas hunkered down next to Otterman. "Who is *she*?"

Otterman's gaze flickered between Walter and his nephew. "The woman who stole my heart—Lady Irene Torsney."

Walter rose and took a step back to carefully assess the small hovel in front of them. Lady Irene Torsney. Certainly, this could not be her abode. Details of last season's scandal came to mind. Lady Irene had been disowned by her papa after she was found to be with child and refused to disclose the name of the scoundrel who had taken her innocence. Her mama hired Bow Street runners to locate her after she went missing. The last reported sighting of the girl was on a mail coach headed for Dover. A flicker of light peeked through the wood slats. There was only one way to find out how she came to be living in the slums of Seven Dials. Walter walked up the steps and reached over Otterman's hunched form. He raised and lowered the brass knocker to rap on the front door three times before leaning back to peer at the window once more. The curtains fluttered and then the door squeaked open.

An exhausted-looking Lady Irene peeked her head out. "Lord Weathersbee. Lord Darlington. I beg you to take your leave."

Walter stepped around Otterman. "Lady Irene, a moment of your time." Before she could close the door, Walter jammed his foot between the door and the frame. "Please."

Boots shuffled behind him. A quick glance behind revealed Otterman breathing down Walter's neck. Lady Irene's dark, shadowed eyes flashed over his shoulder to the man. There was a glimmer of emotion in the woman's gaze Walter couldn't define. Disgust. Desire. Pity. Mayhap a mixture of all three.

She swung the door open. "Very well, but only the two of you may enter."

Walter turned. "Otterman, respect the lady's wishes."

Lady Irene sank into a graceful curtsy as he passed her in the entrance. Her circumstances had certainly changed, but the disowned woman exuded the confidence of a well-bred woman that knew her own mind, much like Henrietta. Only Henrietta had been embraced and protected by the Hadfields, while Lady Irene was left to live in squalor.

Nicholas slid past Otterman and ducked his head as he entered. "My thanks for allowing us an audience."

Both Walter and Nicholas ignored the guttural growl Otterman emitted as the door closed in his face.

Securing the three deadbolts in place, Lady Irene patted the door and spoke through the keyhole. "Charlie, go away!"

"I'm not leaving until they do," Otterman hollered back through the door.

"Grrr." Lady Irene pushed away from the door and led them into a back room.

Walter followed Lady Irene, interested to see what the woman would do next. If she was anything like Henrietta, she would peek through the window to check on Otterman. When she did exactly that, Walter's fate was decided—he was going to assist this woman as best he could.

The house was small, dimly lit, and sparsely furnished. But it was clean. A crib was positioned in front of the fire that illuminated the room. Lady Irene was garbed in a well-worn day dress protected by an apron.

She marched to the fireplace and stoked the dying embers.

Nicholas, quick to assist, said, "Allow me." He took the poker from her hand, crouched, and busied himself rearranging the logs.

Lady Irene peeked into the crib. She reached in and hauled the baby, wrapped in a thick blanket, to her chest. She rocked from side to side and murmured, "Charlie was left penniless. He needs to marry a lady with a fortune. It is why I didn't tell anyone."

Walter needed to hear the truth and have his suspicions confirmed. "Is Lord Otterman the father?"

Head bowed, Lady Irene said, "Aye. I ran away before he found out."

It made no logical sense. Running away placed her babe and herself at risk. Henrietta's voice floated through his mind—*She did it for love.* "Do you love Lord Otterman?" Walter asked.

She sighed and confessed, "Unfortunately, I still do."

Walter glanced at Nicholas, who was shaking his head behind Lady Irene. Lecturing the girl would do no good. She demonstrated a strength that Walter would not have expected from a pampered daughter of an earl. "And yet you are willing to let him go through with his betrothal to Lady Bertha?"

"She has the funds he needs. Please try and understand, my lord. My dowry was insufficient to help out Charlie. I ran away and my papa disowned me." She shifted the babe to the other hip. "Mama's runners found me and brought me here. It is all her pin money can buy."

Interesting that it was Lady Irene's mama who funded the roof of the lady's head and not Otterman. However, if Otterman's financial affairs were as dire as Lady Irene believed, then he did not have the blunt to even afford this pitiful abode. He glanced around at the sparse furnishings. Living in these conditions was a steep price to pay for love.

Lady Irene brushed a tear that had escaped from the corner of her eye. "I didn't think he'd find me. I thought he would have already married. He needs Lady Bertha, not me."

"He found a way to avoid debtors' prison all these months; he can't be totally without funds. It's obvious to me he loves you and you love him." His reply had all the traits of an argument Henrietta might make. She wasn't even present, and Henrietta still was able to influence his thoughts and actions.

"Love doesn't feed mouths, my lord." Lady Irene put the sleeping bundle back into the crib. "Charlie has his tenants to think of. He needs to marry Lady Bertha and to forget about me."

He countered, "Is that what you truly wish?"

She turned to face him. With honest eyes she answered, "No. But wishes are for fools."

"Tell me, if your dowry were enough to cover Lord Otterman's debts, would you agree to marry the man and live a meagre but substantially better life than here in the Dials?"

"Lord Weathersbee, I long ago learnt not to ponder upon what might be and instead to deal with reality in all its harshness." She sighed. "My papa will not pay a penny to the man I marry now. He's disowned me." The baby let out a small cry. Lady Irene rocked the crib and when all was quiet once more, she admitted, "If by some miracle, my papa agreed to pay the dowry, and if it was enough to make Charlie solvent once more, *and* I could save Charlie from the debtors, then I would." She wrapped her arms tight about her waist. "I love the fool."

Nicholas came to stand next to him. "If my uncle is able to arrange matters, will you agree to do your part and marry the man?"

What the devil was his nephew thinking?

"Please don't speak of such absurdity. It will only fuel the false hopes I hold deep in my heart. While my papa holds Lord Weathersbee in high esteem, and it is well known by all that your uncle's skills as a keen negotiator are unparalleled...even so, it would be a great feat to have all of Charlie's affairs set to rights. I can't image anyone being able to complete such a deed."

Nicholas puffed out his chest. "Alas, my lady, you do not know my uncle. There is nothing he cannot accomplish."

Touched by his nephew's faith in him, Walter rested a hand on Nicholas' shoulder. "Allow me to handle this." Walter asked, "Do you trust me?"

The woman searched his features. "Aye."

Grabbing Nicholas by the elbow, Walter gave him a slight shove, prompting the lad to make his way towards the front door before Nicholas made any further promises Walter would have to fulfill. "Then I suggest you prepare to leave this home by week's end." Walter bowed and caught up to his nephew, leaving a stunned Lady Irene behind.

Walter halted on the step and bent down next to the dejected Otterman. "You do not deserve a boon after failing one lady and attempting to trick another. However, I also know it was your papa who was fiscally irresponsible, while you have attempted to rectify his missteps before making your own." Walter straightened. A twinge in his back reminded him of his age. Not as agile as he once was, he rolled to his shoulders and twisted slight to relieve the ache in his lower back. "Argh. Stand up, man."

Confusion plastered on his features, Otterman rose and said, "I blame love for my confounded behavior."

Walter continued, "In love or not, a gentleman should conduct his affairs with honor, not with lies, deception, and secrets. If I assist you out of this mess, you shall promise to conduct yourself as a true gentleman should and bring honor to the Otterman title. Agreed?"

"If you manage such a feat, I shall forever be in your debt."

"It's not your favor I request but your word, Otterman." Walter paused as the man considered his offer and nodded. Satisfied, Walter descended the steps as he said, "You will be required to speak to Lady Bertha directly and apologize, during the morning calling hours. Nicholas shall accompany you to ensure the deed is done."

Otterman nodded but his gaze and form shifted to

Lady Irene's front door. Relieved to see the Darlington coach roll to a stop in front of them, Walter rubbed his aching back, glad he wouldn't have to usher the man too far from the stoop.

Nicholas stepped up to the open coach door. "Otterman, we shall see you home."

Otterman swiveled and approached the vehicle. "My thanks for your assistance, Darlington." He stepped up and flopped on to the forward-facing seat. The entitled fool was sitting in Walter's spot.

Walter replaced his slight frown with a smile as he passed Nicholas. He was grateful for his nephew's company and support this eve. It was a smart move to insist Otterman accompany them. It would do no good to let the man out of their sight until everything had been settled.

Comfortably seated across from Nicholas and Otterman, Walter eyed the man slumped in the corner.

Nicholas leaned forward and motioned for Walter to do the same. "Uncle. If love makes a man behave as such, why would you wish such an affliction for me?"

Otterman had blamed love for his foolish actions. Lady Irene had acted out of love, believing Otterman would be happier and safer without her. Walter himself had made drastic choices in the name of love. Regardless, Nicholas's life would be fuller if he married for love and not for convenience.

"It is a powerful emotion, no doubt." He paused, reordering the words he believed his nephew needed. "I want for you what I was too weak to seek out for myself."

Nicholas snapped back. "You, Uncle, are no weakling. If a life without love was sufficient for you then I shall not require it for myself."

"Nicholas..."

"No, I shall endure the balls, the dancing, the insipid conversations of the weather, but I shall choose my wife-to-be based on sound logic, not an emotion that drives men insane."

Damn. He had failed his brother and his nephew. Walter rubbed his temples. His nephew was as stubborn as an ox once his mind was made up.

Releasing a deep sigh, Walter replied, "As you wish." He'd have to remedy his nephew's views upon love after he was done with Otterman's mess.

Nicholas crossed his arms over his chest and nodded in Otterman's direction. "Love is for fools, and I'm no fool."

CHAPTER NINE

Seated in the front room in her son's townhouse, Henrietta tightened her hold on her dearest friend as Bertha's tears soaked through her sleeve. Bertha's sobs were heart wrenching. The news of Lord Otterman's past deeds and the scandal of a broken engagement were too much for Bertha.

Bertha hiccupped. "You were correct in your suspicions. I should have listened and heeded your advice. Oh, I'm such an idiot."

"You are no such thing. You were deceived..."

"Was I? Or did I simply refuse to face reality. There were clues I ignored, all in the vain hope I might escape the clutches of the greedy men of my family." Faced with the truth, Bertha's open and honest rational thinking had returned. It was a quality they shared and which had bonded them in friendship.

Her friend hadn't exaggerated; the men in Bertha's family cared little about the welfare of women. On an occasion or two, Henrietta had spied the dark tinges upon Bertha's skin when her brothers were denied what they believed was rightfully theirs simply because they were male. Henrietta pulled back, straightened her arms and took a good look at her friend. How had Bertha gone unnoticed all these years? Her pretty brown eyes, set beneath thin shapely brows, shone with intelligence and a hint of cheekiness. Gentlemen of the ton were fools to never recognize the prizes that lay in plain sight. Bertha needed a man who would treasure her unique talents just as George and Walter had appreciated hers. Squeezing Bertha's shoulders, she proclaimed, "I shall find you a husband. A man that is kind, caring, and above all else honest."

Bertha withdrew an embroidered handkerchief from her ridicule and dabbed the tears from her cheek. Hope lit up her features. "A man like Lord Weathersbee?"

Of course, the man would have admirers. Walter was easy on the eyes, wealthy in his own right, and trustworthy. He may not be titled, but women at their age sought companionship and stability, not social status nor love. Disquieted by her thoughts, Henrietta reluctantly asked, "Do you fancy him?"

"Aye." Bertha twisted her hands in her lap. "I have since we were girls. But after the horrific accident that took his family from him, he dedicated himself to raising his brother's boys. And well... I guess I never caught his attention." Bertha raised her head and stared directly at Henrietta. "You are close friends, are you not?"

She took in the eager look in Bertha's clear brown

eyes. Apparently her friend was no longer suffering from heartache. "We were friends, but that was before I was married."

"But you danced with him just last eve. I saw you. Weathersbee never asks a woman to dance except..." Bertha's eyes went wide. "Oh. Oh, my. I apologize, Henrietta. I never meant to imply you were having an affair... ignore me. I'm a ninny. I'm a spinster who obviously should remain firmly cloistered away."

"Stop. Take a deep breath. If you wish, I'll endeavor to discreetly make inquiries on your behalf." It was the least she could do for her friend. To associate with a disowned daughter of a duke had placed Bertha's reputation at risk, but Bertha had lent Henrietta her unfettered support upon her reentrance. Henrietta owed her friend. What harm could it do to inquire if Walter returned Bertha's interest? She was a Hadfield, and it was their duty to seek out the truth.

Miss Marina White twirled away from the far window of the room where she had hidden in order to give her and Bertha some privacy. The scowl on the girl's face sent a shiver down the back of Henrietta's neck. She was feisty.

Bertha turned and asked, "My dear, whatever is the matter?"

Miss White pointed to the window. "Cousin Bertha, the devil himself is walking up the front steps as we speak."

Bertha's brow creased. "The devil? Surely not."

"Indeed, Lord Darlington's the son of Satan all right."

Marina marched across the room and stood before Bertha. "The man is trouble. I suspected as much from our very first meeting, and it was he who accompanied Lord Otterman this morn."

The door to the morning room opened and Morris announced, "Lord Darlington and Lord Weathersbee, my lady."

The gentlemen entered and Miss White tugged at Bertha's arm. Except Bertha's gaze was glued to the door and she remained firmly seated. Miss White's cheeks flushed and a blue vein at the side of the girl's neck pulsed. Lord Darlington's appearance certainly evoked a response within the young lady, one that told Henrietta far more than words.

Henrietta sympathized with the girl, for her own pulse was slightly elevated at the sight of Walter despite his crumpled appearance. "Bertha, if I'm to make the inquiries you wish, it would be best if you took your leave now."

Bertha gave her a wink and smiled. Her friend rose only to sink back down into a curtsy in front of a harried Walter and his nephew. "Lord Weathersbee. Lord Darlington."

Lord Darlington took Bertha's hand. "I'm pleased to see you smiling once more, my lady." The boy's words were meant for Bertha, but his gaze was solely focused on the young lady whose fists were tightly clenched at her sides.

Bertha linked her arm through Miss White's. "A visit with dear Henrietta always restores one's spirits. But alas, it is time for us to take our leave." Bertha stepped around Lord Darlington and addressed Walter, "Will you be attending Lord Thornston's soiree this eve?"

"Unfortunately, I shall have to miss the event this year; however, my nephew shall be present."

"A pity. I know how fond you are of the pianoforte. I hear Lord Thornston's daughter, Lady Emilie, will be playing this eve. It is rumored she is quite accomplished."

Henrietta stiffened at the mention of the pianoforte. She wasn't aware of Walter's preference. She had practiced for hours with him in attendance during the summers they had spent as neighbors in the country. Childhood memories. The silver hair gracing Walter's temples caught her attention. What did she really know of this man? How foolish of her to believe he had remained the same all these years. Walter hadn't been her boon companion in years. She'd have to rediscover the man.

It appeared that Henrietta was not the only one who took note of Bertha's comment. At the mention of Lady Emilie, Lord Darlington leaned in to listen closer. In turn, Miss White's eyes narrowed at the boy with a hint of jealousy. The ebb and flow of energy that surrounded the couple was highly volatile and highly entertaining. Lord Darlington and Miss White were perfect for each other.

Bertha shifted to face Henrietta and asked, "Will you be joining us this eve?"

Behind Bertha, Walter's nose scrunched up, his lips puckered, and his brow lowered as one eye semi-closed. It was the most confounding yet comical facial expressions she'd ever witnessed. What in the blazes was he doing? If he was trying to prompt her to decline, why hadn't he simply shaken his head or tugged on his right ear—their childhood signal for the word *no*?

Swallowing a giggle, Henrietta replied, "I don't believe I will be in attendance. My dear daughter-in-law has requested I stay in tonight and keep her company, now that she is near term."

Before Bertha could respond, Miss White bobbed a quick curtsy and whisked her cousin out of the room, but not before darting Lord Darlington one last glare.

Hands on her hips, Henrietta waited for the sound of the clattering of carriage wheels out front before rounding on the man who nearly had her in fits of laughter at the most inappropriate times. "Walter Weathersbee." She waved her hand in circles in front her face as she mimicked his earlier facial expressions. "What was all that about?"

Lord Darlington, who she'd nearly forgotten was in the room, let out a chuckle and then whirled about, pretending to inspect the painting of Hadfield Hall that sat upon the nearest wall with great interest.

"I'm certain I have no inkling as to what you are referring to." Walter ran a hand over his face and rubbed the back of his neck. A reddish tinge colored his cheek bones. Walter was a terrible liar.

Placing her hands back on her hips, she asked, "Why did you not wish for me to attend Thornton's soiree?"

His gaze flickered to his nephew and then back to

her. "I believe it only fair you forgo tonight's entertainment to assist me this eve. We need to work on devising a plan to rectify Otterman's mangled affairs." He grinned and added, "After all, it was you who originally requested I involve myself in the matter."

About half-way through his long-winded explanation, Henrietta lost focus and stared at his moving lips. Lips that were rather inviting. Her mind replacing the words he spoke with ones of her own—*I want to spend time alone with you. To have you in my arms. To feel your lips upon mine.* Heavy foot falls pierced through her wayward thoughts.

Landon appeared in the threshold of the drawing-room door. When would the boy ever learn to tread lightly?

"Morris informed me we had visitors." Landon scanned the room. "Where are Lady Bertha and Miss White?"

At the sight of her son's dark scowl directed at Walter, Henrietta answered, "On their way back to Bertha's residence, I believe."

Landon's lips thinned. "Weathersbee. Darlington. What brings you here today?"

Lord Darlington stepped forward. "We came to provide you with an update regarding Otterman."

"Landon, why don't you escort Lord Darlington to your study, where the two of you can discuss matters." She didn't give her son a chance to rebuke. Instead, she turned Landon about by the shoulders and gave him a solid shove towards the door.

Lord Darlington, smart lad that he was, picked up on her scheme and walked slightly behind Landon to skillfully guide her son out into the hall.

Grinning, Henrietta twirled and came face-to-face with Walter. A rather handsomely disheveled Walter with a finger tugging at his cravat. Henrietta's stomach knotted as his warm brown eyes bored into hers. Unaccustomed to Walter's direct stares, Henrietta shifted and tugged at her skirts. Blast the man! How had Walter Weathersbee of all people ruffled her normally unflappable nerves? Uncertain she would be able to continue to stand under his watchful attention, Henrietta gracefully settled herself upon the empty settee. Mustering all the bravado she could, she lifted her chin and asked, "With what exactly do you need my assistance?"

Ignoring the comfortable chair next to the settee, Walter sat beside her. "I'm in need of your guidance regarding how best to handle Lady Irene Torsney's reentrance into the ton."

"Who in the blazes is Lady Irene Torsney?"

Walter shook his head. "Did I not mention Lady Irene is the woman Otterman will be marrying?"

"No, you did not." Henrietta frowned as information on the lady came to mind. Lady Irene Torsney. Daughter of the Earl of Tinsmore. Disowned after refusing to disclose the name of the man who got her with child. "The ton is notorious for shunning women who are embroiled in scandal." Walter's knee brushed her thigh. Her thoughts scattered at the innocent touch. Clutching her hands together in her lap, she waited until her pulse returned to a steady pace. "Marrying Otterman does not guarantee her reentrance into society."

"Exactly. However, for the sake of Otterman's heir, it is important that the Earl and Countess of Otterman are well received and accepted back into the fold once more."

How insightful of Walter to consider the ramifications that might ensue for the poor child. Otterman's heir should not suffer as a result of his papa's idiocy. She glanced up at Walter and gave him a half-smile. They had a task that required them to work together in unison like they used to do when they were children. Familiar camaraderie sent warmth radiating down her body to the spot where Walter's knee connected them.

Clasping her hands in her lap, she said, "What Lady Irene needs is the full endorsement of an untarnished, well-respected matron of the ton." She lowered her gaze to his chest as the shame of her own disownment hit her. Even to this day, her family refused to acknowledge her. On the rare occasions when she was present at an event where her siblings were in attendance, they showed no remorse and gave her the cut direct. It was the stout support of her fellow PORFs that had provided Henrietta solace and the courage to reenter society.

Walter reached out and covered her hands with one of his own. "That may be, but Lady Irene will need you, Henrietta. A magnificent and brave woman who understands how to navigate and regain the good graces of the ton."

"You think I've accomplished such a feat?"

"Your salver is full with invitations. You are never in want of company at any event I've seen you attend."

Henrietta trusted Walter, but she couldn't disclose the existence of PORFs. Instead, she opted for a more indirect explanation. "That is due to the kindness and generosity extended to me by my dear niece-in-law. The Archbrokes have always maintained a level of unparalleled connections and influence."

Walter's lips twisted into a smile that sparked the passion-filled sensations she'd suppressed. "Henrietta, your dear George was never one to strictly adhere to the rules. I'm fully aware your connection to the Archbroke family dates back further than your niece's recent marriage into the family."

She blinked twice and studied Walter's features. He wasn't lying. Why would George have shared with Walter, a gentleman with no ties to the crown, the Hadfields' generations-old secret? Henrietta's confusion was only further muddled at the sight of Walter's lips curled into a flirtatious grin and the alluring appearance of fine lines at the corners of his smiling eyes.

Walter squeezed her hand. "I see you don't believe how that could be."

She leaned forward, never letting her gaze drop from his. "And I'm still owed an explanation as to exactly how your friendship with George came about."

Bridging the gap between them until they were inches apart, Walter replied, "And I agreed to divulge all my secrets once my dear nephew is happily engaged, did I not?"

Her heart was racing. This very mature, very controlled version of Walter had her on edge. "Aye, that was the arrangement. However..."

Walter rested a warm hand upon her knee, halting her speech. "Henrietta, I shall share everything with you as promised...at a later date. For now, we must combat the scandal that is about to ensue in order for Lady Bertha to find a suitable husband."

"A husband such as yourself?" She couldn't resist the opening.

Walter pulled his hand away. "No. Whatever gave you the idea I shared a fondness for Lady Bertha?"

"Mayhap the lady has an interest in you." Argh. She had promised Bertha to be subtle.

"Then it is certainly imperative we find her a suitable match."

"Why are you so eager to have Bertha wed?"

"Because I believe you were correct that Miss White is perfect for your nephew, and the chit is extremely loyal to her own detriment. She won't wed until Lady Bertha is happily settled."

"How do you know of such things?"

"Servants talk, and I have my own network to provide me information and gossip."

It wasn't her imagination; Walter had placed an emphasis on network. She'd have to extract the man's secrets sooner rather than later.

"Shall I make arrangements for us all to dine this eve?" Henrietta stood and walked over to the pull.

Walter rose and before she could summon Morris, he

was mere inches away. "It is my understanding Landon and his dear wife make a habit of dining in private of late. I would not like to disrupt your routine."

Goodness, the man was well informed.

He arched a brow at her. "Perhaps we could dine— just the two of us."

She no longer detested the idea of eating alone, often opting to dine in her chambers. But recently the lack of company frequently resulted in her pecking at her food and discarding it half eaten. Not that she didn't have a stone or two to spare. "Are you suggesting I allow you to sneak into my parlor, as you did as a boy to enjoy a plate of sweets?"

"I am. I am indeed." His eyes glimmered with desire.

With a smile, Henrietta answered, "Very well. I shall see you later this eve."

Walter bowed and disappeared, leaving Henrietta alone with her mind awhirl. What was the man's favored sweet dish? With her forefinger pressed against her lips, she smiled—bread and butter pudding! She would simply request Cook to add a plate of the treat to her tray this eve. As she neared the kitchens, she was struck with the idea to have a bowl of syllabub also added. Her cheeks burned red as she made the request that Cook didn't even bat an eye at. He simply shooed her from the blazing hot room, and Henrietta practically skipped back to her rooms pondering over the all the delicious and decadent ideas of how to share the whipped-cream dessert with Walter.

CHAPTER TEN

Ouch! The toe of Walter's boot hit the stone wall. His depth perception was askew in the darkness. Barely enough moonlight to see his own nose. Not as nimble as he once was, instead of hopping the garden wall, he swung one leg over and then the next. Seated, he searched his surroundings to gain his bearings before making the terrifying attempt of entering the wing assigned to Henrietta. He had spent the afternoon at Neale & Sons, seated at his desk and haunted by the wispy crackle of George's voice. *She deserves happiness, Walter; promise you won't fail as I have in leaving her.* Walter had pondered for years as to why George had been taken from this earth at a young age. More often than not, those moments coincided with his morose thoughts of how his own family members had departed before their time. And after all these years, Walter still could not shake the dead man's words from his conscience. Haunted by a gnawing obligation to fulfill his promise, Walter had remained close by, always at the ready to assist but hidden in the shadows. Now that he had been pushed out of the dark, he was challenged with deciding how to go on. How was he to fulfill his promise and see to Henrietta's happiness—and perhaps his own? Mayhap dining in private with the woman was the first step. Although he wasn't certain he'd leave with his sanity intact. Thirty minutes alone with her had proven to be a supreme challenge of his will power. He had been inches away from kissing her soft, inviting lips. He was still undecided as to whether he was a fool for not pursuing a life-long fantasy or a saint for exercising such self-control. An evening alone with Henrietta would prove which.

Pushing off the wall, Walter crept to the window illuminated with candlelight. He pressed his ear to the glass plane. The second half of George's demand—that Walter promise to never leave Henrietta—froze his movements. If he dared to kiss Henrietta this eve, leaving her might well be an impossibility. Loving her from afar had been torture. But to declare his affection for her to all and sundry petrified him.

The crackle of the fire inside broke his train of thought. He waited for any indication Henrietta might not be alone. Silence. He shouldn't delay a moment longer; the Network and Landon's own footmen probably kept close guard on the family quarters. Walter raised his knuckles and rapped on the window. The latch clicked open and Henrietta's flushed face appeared as she raised the window sash. "I was beginning to question whether or not you were going to make an appearance."

Relief swept through him as he slipped through the window. In an effort to distract himself from her tempting pursed lips, he pulled out his pocket watch. "Am I late? Do you not dine at nine?" She remained close, too tempting with her chin tilted up.

With a slight frown creasing her brow, Henrietta said, "I do, but most families dine at eight."

"But you do not run a traditional household nor adhere to societal norms." He moved to remove his outer garments, but Henrietta reached up and placed her hands on his shoulders. Even through all the layers of clothing, he shivered. She divested him of his hat, then his great coat, and took his gloves. Without a word she walked across the room.

Mesmerized by the sway of her hips, he remained stock still. She made her way over to the settee, turned, and bent to place the articles of clothing on the side table. Without pause, she continued on to the quaint dining table set with dinner for two. Without footmen to attend to them, he should have followed her. He ought to be standing next to Henrietta instead of ogling her perfectly plump rear covered in glorious indigo silk.

Rushing forward to retrieve the chair for her, he reached her with a moment to spare. "I wanted to thank you for agreeing to this unorthodox meeting."

His heart raced either from his quick pace to reach her or from merely being alone with the woman. He closed his eyes and inhaled deeply. A mistake. Henrietta's signature scent of violets hit him, bringing to mind the time they sat high up in a tree limb, him with his back pressed up against the trunk and hers pressed up against his chest. He remembered resting his chin on her shoulder pretending to read over her shoulder but in fact his eyes were closed. Knowing it would be the last time they would scale the tree together, he had savored every moment, memorized the smells, the sounds, and the feel of her between his legs. He opened his eyes to find her head tilted up towards him.

"I'm anything but orthodox, as you have already noted." The cheeky curve of her lips highlighted the faint lines that came with age. Lines that tempted him, begging him to come closer. To be seen.

They hadn't yet dined.

To hell with propriety.

Three decades of restraint fell to the wayside. He placed a hand on the back of her chair and bent down, lowering until her breath brushed over his mouth. She stole his breath away. To his astonishment, she twisted and reached up to wrap a hand about the back of his neck. With a gentle pressure, she drew him down to her. No innocent brushing of lips from Henrietta. He relished the taste of her as their tongues collided and her fingers weaved through his hair. Weak from their kiss, he dropped to his knees. Unwilling to relinquish the lips of the woman he'd loved for the majority of his life, he cupped her face and grazed her bottom lip with a long stroke of his tongue. She leaned in and captured his prying tongue between her lips. Henrietta's kisses were passionate, full of flavor and excitement, just like her.

A soft mewl escaped Henrietta, and he pulled back. "We should dine..."

Henrietta grinned and bent to kiss him once more. This time encircling him with both arms, she hugged him to her. Her lush breasts pressed against his chest. Cursing the clothing that separated them, Walter regained his strength and rose, pulling her up with him as they waltzed backward toward the settee. Henrietta fell atop of him as the back of his calves hit the edge of the furniture.

Settled on top of him, she giggled. "I shouldn't be surprised, but you are an extraordinary kisser. Is there nothing you do poorly?"

There were a multitude of tasks he underperformed, but with all the blood vacating his mind, he was left with only the ability to give her a non-verbal response. He raised both eyebrows and shrugged, which evoked another giggle from Henrietta. He ceased her laughter with a kiss that had her sighing a moan as he nibbled down her neck.

His fingers searched for the ends of two ties that should release Henrietta from the dratted dress that covered her beautiful body. Instead, his fingers met with a row of hard round objects. Buttons! It had been some time since he last dallied with a lady. Of course, fashions had to have changed, making it harder to undress a woman.

Walter removed his lips from Henrietta's and

growled, "Damn the woman who designed this blasted gown."

Henrietta reeled back, her features filled with mirth. She stared down at him, "Surely you wouldn't really condemn my dear beloved daughter-in-law, Emma."

"Emma? I was under the assumption..." He sealed his lips shut. He wasn't supposed to know of the Hadfield family ties to PORFs or the Network. Attempting to recover his mistake he quickly said, "Nay. I'd never wish ill upon Christopher's lovely wife." He tapped the buttons and added, "However, I shall have a word with her about these gowns upon her return."

Henrietta's narrowed gaze searched his features. She placed her hands flat against his chest and pushed herself up. She rolled to her feet with a grace that bellied her years to stand over him with her hands on her hips once more. "How is it you are so certain that she and Christopher shall return?"

Adjusting his crumpled clothing back to rights, Walter sat upright and patted the cushion next to him. Releasing a deep sigh, Henrietta obliged and sank down next to him. Taking her hand in his, he weaved his fingers with hers. He stared at their entwined fingers for a moment and relief washed over him as Henrietta curled her fingers over his.

Face-to-face, Walter confessed, "I came across a number of documents—trade agreements that Christopher was in the midst of drafting, complex arrangements that could only be completed if he were to return."

RACHEL ANN SMITH

"Trade contracts, you say. Who were the parties involved?"

The details were not for him to share. He hated denying her questions. But the agreements were incomplete, and it would not be in good faith to disclose particulars that were still in negotiations. He remained quiet and shook his head.

"Your features would indicate you do not agree with the terms."

He should ignore her remark. Damn, he'd never be able to deny Henrietta. Walter relented. "It is not that I disagree... However, there are a multitude of considerations to take into account when dealing with foreign merchants, and yet, these agreements would have a significant impact upon the livelihoods of many here, some now directly linked to your own family."

"I married a barrister and raised two. That, my dear lord, was a cleverly constructed response that told me nothing I didn't already know." Henrietta's disappointment was clear. There would be no more kisses. She untangled her hand from his and stood. He followed her back to the dining table and sat across from her. They both removed the silver covers and silently assessed their plates.

When she wouldn't meet his gaze, he asked, "Have you changed your mind? Would you prefer to dine alone?"

"No." She shook her head and with her brows knitted, continued, "I know it's unfair of me to compare, but George never withheld information from me. I had hoped...well, I'd thought perhaps... What I'm trying to say is I'd like for us..."

He hated her struggle to define what it was she wanted. To add levity, he finished her third attempt for her. "To be close friends like we were prior to you running off and marrying George."

"Yes, exactly." She beamed him a smile.

Before she eloped with George, they were more than just close friends. He had made it no secret, he was infatuated and in love with her. She had even hinted a time or two that she too shared such feelings. But neither of them were brave enough to confess or act upon those undercurrents that still existed. He picked up his knife and fork and cut into the piece of lukewarm chicken.

"Agreed. We shall simply begin where we left off all those years ago." He winked at her, causing color to return to her cheeks once more.

At least she wasn't tossing him out. He might still have a chance this eve to formulate a plan to divest Henrietta of her gown and perform all the illicit acts he'd imagined doing with her before she ran off with George.

CHAPTER ELEVEN

*F*ocused on the congealed chicken on her plate, Henrietta waited for her pulse to resume its normal even pace. Decades had gone by since she had last experienced the heart-stopping effect Walter had on her. As a lad, his enthusiasm and clever insight had set her heart and mind racing. In their youth, on multiple occasions—too many to count—they had set out and solved mysteries that at the time were deemed to be life altering. Her lips curled at the memory, at the numerous preposterous hypotheses they had formulated as to how animals reproduced. Countless hours of monitoring the farmer's bull that more often than not stood alone in the corner of the paddock.

Walter broke her reverie. "Pray tell, what is so amusing?"

"I was merely recalling the summer we failed to solve the mystery as to how cow Belle managed to get her belly full."

"Ah, that was a rather long summer." Walter lifted his fork loaded with cold chicken and popped it into his mouth.

Henrietta stared at the lips that caused her blood to stir once more. She lowered her eyes to her plate, but her appetite fled her. Knots gathered in her stomach as George's visage formed amongst her meal. The blood drained from her face.

The scrape of a chair alerted her to Walter's movements. Kneeling beside her, he reached for her hands. She snatched them back from him.

"Henrietta. What is the matter?"

Head shaking, she mumbled, "I shouldn't have... We shouldn't be..."

Walter rested his hand upon her knee and squeezed to gain her full attention. "I apologize for my advances. It was not my intent to cause you distress—ever." His gaze was filled with remorse. Walter rose and walked over to where she had placed his outer garments.

She rushed to him. "Walter." What was she to say? She didn't want him to leave.

George had always understood her need to be a mama first. Her devotion to her boys and her oath as a PORF meant they came before all else. Having never been tempted by another's kisses, Henrietta had been blissfully content—until now. Long ago, there had been fleeting moments when Walter had held her hand and led her about that she'd imagined kissing the man, but that had all occurred in her imagination. Her girlish thoughts paled in comparison to the searing kisses she had experienced with Walter earlier.

Slowly pivoting, Walter faced her with masked features. "I should take my leave. I..."

"Please don't go." Henrietta rested her hand on his arm.

Walter had always stirred within her a powerful urge to leap to action before considering the ramifications. She also had unfailing faith he would never let her come to harm, which stemmed from an unexplainable feeling deep within her from the day they met—her perched in a tree, him lost in the woods. During their childhood years, he had relentlessly pushed her to question the boundaries she imposed upon herself. And earlier, in his arms, she wanted to smash the invisible walls she had erected about her, explore the invigorating surge of energy that had once again resurfaced.

"My dear Henrietta. Tell me what it is you want from me."

"I..." The turmoil within her was mirrored in Walter's gaze. How was she to articulate these new confounding thoughts and emotions, when she hadn't muddled through them herself? "I wish for us to become reacquainted as we were once."

Walter's amiable smile returned. "You wouldn't know this, but I often ask myself 'what would George do or say' and have done so for years. He was a remarkable man and a loyal friend. I would never wish to betray his memory."

"Do you believe he'd condone our...earlier actions?"

Never before had she skirted topics. She preferred to be direct to avoid misunderstandings, but the words to admit to having a desire for a man other than George caught in her throat.

"I've thought long and hard about the matter—for years, in fact." Walter squeezed the muscles at the back of his neck. "His voice echoes in my thoughts."

"What do you believe he would say?"

"I can't be certain. However, he extracted from me a promise to see to your happiness." He rested his hand upon her waist. "Did my kisses bring you joy?"

Her heart leapt at his touch. She leaned in closer and raised her lips mere inches from his and rasped, "Yes."

Dipping his head, Walter leaned in to press his lips to hers. It was a sweet, gentle brush of his mouth. His tongue slipped between her lips, entangling with her own. Unlike the passionate kisses earlier, this kiss was languid and filled with a depth of emotion that rocked Henrietta to her core. She didn't want it to end. Encircling his waist with her arms, she pressed herself closer. The cool metal button of his jacket pressed into her chest and she snaked her hand between them to divest Walter of his clothing. At her back, Walter's fingers fumbled with the buttons of her dress, and then stilled.

Walter released a half groan, half chuckle. "Blasted contraptions."

"I seem to be out of practice."

Walter stilled at her words and pulled back. "We don't..."

She placed a forefinger to his lips. "My decision remains unaltered. Yours?"

He shook his head, and she boldly turned her back to him. Walter released each button. The material of her gown loosened, and she breathed easier. The gentle pressure of his fingertips against her back stirred the shock waves that had unnerved her as a girl. Henrietta held her breath in anticipation as her gown fell to the ground. She shifted to turn once more, but Walter held her still as he tugged on the ties of her stays. Freed from the boned bodice, Henrietta's lungs filled with air. The hem of her shift grazed the back of her calves. Walter removed the last barrier swiftly and she raised her arms to assist. She hadn't stood naked before a man in a very long time. The warmth from her cheeks spread throughout and as the cool night air hit her skin, she slowly swiveled to face the man she'd shared a kinship with as a child but was now intent to explore as a man.

Absolutely breathtaking. Walter lowered his gaze to memorize every inch of Henrietta's glorious body. Unforgettable. He clenched Henrietta's shift in his hand while attempting to remain still. The woman of his dreams lifted her hands to unbutton his jacket. She had lowered her guard, which was a rarity, and gave him full access to undress her. He wanted to do the same, but it was extremely difficult to refrain from touching her. His breath hitched and the soft linen material dropped from his hand as she smoothed her palms over his chest, divesting him of his jacket. His arm brushed against the side of her full bosom as he pulled it through the sleeve. The flare of excitement and desire in Henrietta's eyes echoed his own wishes.

Deftly she loosened his cravat but before she could tug it free he stilled her hands. "Please take a seat, my lady."

Henrietta glanced back at the settee and then sank down as if she was fully clothed and about to offer him tea and not her delicious body. Walter sank to his knees. Henrietta was offering him a lifetime of fantasies, but knowing how his kisses had perturbed her earlier, he was determined Henrietta would not regret her decision to further their relationship.

He cupped her knees and gently parted her legs. A blush kissed the tops of Henrietta's breasts and cheeks. Every heartbeat he anxiously awaited her command to stop, and when her lips curved into a smile, Walter swallowed his fears and seized the opportunity. His hands skimmed the tops of her thighs, pausing at the pretty lace garter that was adorned with pink bows. "You've always had a fondness for pink."

"Have I?" Her lazy smile transformed into a sensual, teasing grin. "I'll warn you, not all my preferences have stayed the same. Have yours?"

"I remain partial to pink also." He rubbed his thumb over the soft tender skin of her inner thigh. "Have you outgrown your abhorrence to being tickled?"

Henrietta squirmed in her seat but did not dislodge

his hold upon her. Edging his fingers closer to his prize, he spied the small bead of moisture that told him her body was ready—but was her heart? His gaze wavered between the delicious delight before him and her sparkling eyes. He inched his hand closer to her slit, and when the tip of his finger grazed against the edge, Henrietta's eyes fluttered closed. He replaced his fingers with the tip of his tongue and circled the delicate hood over her core. Henrietta's muscles tensed beneath his palms as he continued to pleasure her with alternating long broad strokes and quick flickers of his tongue. He savored the flavors that were entirely Henrietta; a sweet, salty mix. The heady scent of her filled the air as he buried his face between her lush thighs. Intoxicating as her soft moans.

Walter shifted and firmly drew her intimate bud between his lips which were covered with in her juices. Henrietta's moans increased in intensity, encouraging him to continue. Her inner muscles clenched around the tips of his two fingers placed at her entrance.

Henrietta weaved her fingers through his hair and tugged. "Oh, god, don't stop."

The possibility of halting what they had begun was remote. Being physically intimate with Henrietta only strengthened the strong emotional bond she had held on him. Warm satisfaction engulfed him—a reward for his patience all these years. Slipping his fingers in her passage, Walter resolved to give Henrietta a night of pure pleasure that would haunt her nights like it was surely going to reoccur in his dreams. He pushed deeper into her, searching for the elusive spot that would make her come undone. Suckling and thrusting his fingers in and out until finally Henrietta arched her back and called out his name. The strain in his breeches reminded him of his own needs, but they would have to wait. There was no need to rush Henrietta.

He raised his head and smiled at the pink flush that graced the woman's beautiful body and face. "Henrietta..."

She released her grip on his hair. "Yes?"

He arched a brow, like he had as a boy when she begged for him to continue pushing her on the tree swing. "Ready?" Not waiting for her reply, he dipped his head and skimmed the tip of his tongue over her sensitive core over and over until she was writhing and moaning his name once more.

Walter rose and picked up Henrietta's limp and sated body. She curled into him, but her movements were tentative.

He peered down at her. "No regrets?"

She shook her head but did not meet his gaze. "None."

Walter carried her through the connecting door into her dark bed chamber. With no fire lit, there was a chill in the air, and he hugged Henrietta's closer. Instead of seeking out his warmth, she stiffened in his arms. A sharp ache radiated through his chest. Henrietta may have denied having regrets, but her actions said otherwise.

He strode to the large, canopied bed and laid Henrietta upon the mattress. She quickly ducked under the coverlet and pulled it up to her chin. Walter turned to leave, intending to retrieve a candle. It was unlikely she'd invite him to join her.

Henrietta called out, "Don't leave."

Walter halted with one foot through the threshold. He looked over his shoulder.

Henrietta's smile was timid, unlike her normal bold, daring grin. "Please."

The ache in his chest deepened. He nodded and said, "I shall return."

He scanned the empty room. His pulse sped up as he spied the pile of silk and linen next to the settee. He had waited years—decades—to have the opportunity to be with Henrietta in an intimate manner. Now that he'd experienced the taste of her upon his tongue, his lungs filled with her unique scent, his heart thrumming with the sounds of her desire, he was uncertain he could slip back into loving her from the shadows. For the two years Henrietta was in mourning, Walter watched as she built barriers around her. She avoided social events, restricted visitors, and devoted herself to raising her boys and fulfilling her oath as a PORF. Those walls of defense were steadfast, yet she had allowed him to breach them this eve, and he needed to know why.

Grabbing a candle from the abandoned dining table, he shielded the flame and walked back to Henrietta's bed chamber determined to extract the answers that would determine his future.

Striding directly to the fireplace, he glanced over at Henrietta, who gave him a broad smile. Her outward display of bravery bolstered his own courage.

The sound of his knees cracking echoed through the room as he squatted to ignite the tinder in the fireplace. "Henrietta, there is something..." The flame flickered as a whoosh of air brushed against the back of his neck. He turned to see Henrietta throwing back the sheets in a flurry and rushing to his side.

Naked and kneeling next to him, Henrietta cupped his face, "Are you well?"

The concern in her eyes gave him pause. "Why are you inquiring about my health?" He reached for her and she hugged him tight. Wrapping his arms about her as he stood, Walter said, "Let's get you back under the covers."

She tightened her hold on him. "Will you join me?"

How he desperately wanted to say yes, but his instincts told him to remain patient and give her time. They walked back to the bed and Henrietta hopped up and scuttled back under the covers. Out of habit, he tucked the sheets about her like he used to with his nephews and niece. He sat upon the bed one foot on the floor and the other bent at the knee.

She reached for his hand and he threaded his fingers with hers. "Walter. I want..."

He waited for her to continue, and when she didn't, he said, "For years I've watched you skillfully avoid the attention of men." Summoning all the courage he could, he asked, "Why me? Why now?"

"Why you..." Henrietta shifted to sit upright and pulled the sheet up to cover her generous chest. "You are the only man, Walter Weathersbee, who has ever caused my mind to cease fixating on what needs to be done and focus on me—my wants, my wishes. Your kisses make me feel desired and cherished." She leaned forward, exposing the tops of her breasts. "And now that my boys are happily married, I believe I am ready to see to my own happiness."

His self-restraint was fraying by the second. He wanted to strip out of his clothes and fulfill all his fantasies, but Henrietta had used the words *I believe*, not *I am*, and those two additional words were enough to plant a seed of doubt in his mind. He didn't want to leave, yet he couldn't act upon his desires with a clear conscience. He shifted to sit next to her and wrapped an arm about her.

Henrietta snugged closer. "I gather you have decided I'm not to receive more kisses."

"Not tonight, my dear."

"Tomorrow, then." Her cheeky response surprised him.

"Aye, mayhap tomorrow." He sensed her smiling. Walter took pleasure at having made her happy and held her tight.

She rested her head against his shoulder, and it wasn't long before her breathing evened out. Gently extracting himself from her bed, Walter pressed a kiss to her temple and positioned the covers over her bare shoulders. Looking down at the woman who owned his heart, the truth hit him—he needed to be prepared and willing to also stop placing the needs of his family above his own.

CHAPTER TWELVE

*U*nwilling to leave the safe cocoon of her bed, Henrietta shimmied down under the linens and pressed a pillow over her head. She had slept soundly until the first streaks of dawn peeked through the curtains. Walter had gone, leaving the space next to her cold and empty. She groaned as remorse settled in. Walter had aroused responses within her that overpowered her senses. She panicked. It was no secret that he had lain with skilled courtesans and experienced widows, while she had only ever been intimate with her late husband. Ashamed of her lack of courage, she sighed and rolled over to face the entrance to her bedchamber. The sharp click-clack of heels signaled her daughter-in-law's arrival. No more lingering in bed pondering about what could have been a night of decadent pleasure.

Having missed the morning meal, Henrietta had two choices: feign illness or face Bronwyn's inquisition directly. It was doubtful Bronwyn would believe her

119

claims of exhaustion. Although it was partially the truth. Her aging body was unaccustomed to the heightened rate at which her heart beat due to Walter's attentions last night. Rolling out of bed, Henrietta padded over to her chest of drawers to quickly retrieve and don a night gown. Her skin prickled as the material skimmed over her. Memories of Walter's palms running up her sides and then cupping her bosoms caused her nipples to harden. She returned to the bed, reached for her robe, and slipped it on. Now was not the time for reliving the intimate moments of the prior evening. Henrietta moved to the windows and pulled back the drapes. Daylight streamed into the room. Good gracious, it was nearing midday.

Striding through her bed chamber, she rolled her shoulders back preparing for an onslaught of questions from Bronwyn. She made it to the threshold before Bronwyn, garbed in a delightful light-green day dress, waltzed in with a tray. "Why did you not join us this morn?"

The concern on her daughter-in-law's features was touching. Not having birthed a daughter, Henrietta now had two. Albeit one resided on the other side of the world. Bronwyn's fierce need for independence and natural instinct to assist others meant they often thought alike, which most of the time was an advantage but might prove a nuisance that day.

"I simply decided to remain abed and rest a while longer." Henrietta frowned as she seated herself opposite Bronwyn at the table. When had the servants removed the remnants of her meal with Walter? More importantly, which of the servants had performed the task? She glanced over to the settee. Her gown and her other arti-cles of clothing were also missing. The staff were extremely loyal to Landon, but they had been Henrietta's supporters first and for many more years.

Smiling, Bronwyn picked up the pot and poured a steady stream of hot tea into a cup. "Landon informed me of Lord Weathersbee's rather intriguing visit with the recently rediscovered Lady Irene." She held out the cup and saucer for Henrietta.

"My thanks, dear." Henrietta accepted the tea and set it down upon the table. "Did my son inform you that the lady is to wed Otterman?" While she was an advocate for love matches, there were exceptions to every rule. Both Lady Irene and Otterman had claimed love was the cause for their ill-conceived decisions. But Henrietta believed love gave one strength and wisdom. Her sons' and Theo's marriages were proof that her hypothesis was correct.

Smoothing out her napkin in her lap, Bronwyn said, "Aye, he did. He also said Lord Weathersbee intended to request your assistance in seeing to Lady Irene's return into the fold of the ton." Henrietta waited for Bronwyn to state her opinion regarding the crazed notion, that she of all the ladies of the ton could manage to pull off such a grand feat. Instead her daughter-in-law's gaze shifted over to the settee and then back to Henrietta. "Will you provide Lord Weathersbee with what he seeks?"

Either Bronwyn had been informed of Walter's visit last night or the girl was far too insightful. Regardless, there was no hiding Henrietta's heated cheeks. She lifted her cup to her lips, lips that had been thoroughly kissed by Walter, and sipped on the tepid tea. Would she be brazen enough to lure Walter back into her bed? A giddy feeling erupted within her and she smiled behind her cup. Yes. Yes, she would.

Bronwyn's brows met in the center as she leaned forward and rested her elbows upon the table to assess Henrietta's features. With a shrug, Bronwyn answered the question herself. "Your smile tells me you are considering the matter." Brows still set in a frown, Bronwyn reached for a slice of toast. "What a coup it would be, to have Lady Irene—a lady who had been disowned, banished even..." She picked up her butter knife and waved it about in the air. "A woman who birthed a child out of wedlock, then married a gentleman well and truly in dun territory." Bronwyn let out a sigh. "Ahh. To have her relaunched into society with an aplomb that ensured her place in society, not relegated to the fringes..." Bronwyn fixed her gaze upon Henrietta and said, "Ooh, what I would give to see that!"

Henrietta sputtered as she returned her teacup to its saucer. "When you phrase it like that, that would be rather remarkable."

"I've not met the woman." To Henrietta's relief, Bronwyn laid down the knife. "Let's invite her for tea so we can devise a plan."

Her daughter-in-law was mad if she believed they could manage such a task. "My dear, such a triumph would be... well, near impossible."

"Bah! We are Neales. If Lady Irene had the courage

to face a life of misery and squalor rather than give up the name of the sod that got her belly full, then I believe—with, of course, the assistance of Cousin Theo—we could devise a reentry that will leave the ton no choice but to embrace her, to forgive and forget past deeds."

Henrietta shook her head. "You, my dear, have been confined in this house too long." She took in Bronwyn's flushed face and sparkling eyes. Henrietta recognized that guilty, mischievous look. "You have been reading those horrid Radcliffe novels, have you not?"

"How can you refer to them as horrid? I believe them to be splendid works of fiction. Clever, confident women outsmarting men. The heroines remind me of…"

Henrietta arched a brow. When Bronwyn didn't complete her sentence, she said, "Lady Irene is no fictional character. And the gossip of the ton is a far scarier living creature than the monster described in the newest gothic fiction penned by… oh, what is the name of that woman…"

"Mary Shelley!" Bronwyn scanned the room. "You have the book—*Frankenstein*?"

Of course she had a copy, along with every volume printed by Minerva Press. "Aye. I shall allow you to borrow it on one condition. That you promise to cease confusing fiction with reality."

"I don't believe it is *I* who is confused." Bronwyn rose from the table and padded over to the door to leave. One hand on the door handle, she turned and said, "I'll have Morris deliver an invitation to Lady Irene and Theo for tea this afternoon—that should allow you plenty of time to dress and rejoin us in the here and now."

Henrietta took a bite of her toast as the door clicked closed. What in tarnation was Bronwyn's departing statement all about? Oh, her daughter-in-law was a force to be reckoned with when she chose to be. It was one of the many fine qualities Henrietta admired about Bronwyn, and an absolute requirement to have married her stubborn firstborn.

With no appetite for food, Henrietta took one last sip of tea and then shuffled back to bed and slipped between the cool sheets. All alone, the swirl of emotions that had plagued her in the early hours of the day returned. Images from the eve before taunted her. She had lain upon the settee, naked. A willing participant as all the while, Walter avoided her attempts to divest him of his clothing. He pleasured her until she was limp and fully sated and then he stopped, sensing doubts she had buried deep within. She repositioned her pillow over her head to block out the light and replayed the events of the prior evening over and over in her mind.

Walter had mentioned his promise to George to ensure her happiness. Were his attentions out of duty not desire? Attempting to reconcile memories from their childhood and the man who stirred passions within her, Henrietta let out a low growl. It was so confusing. Walter had a way of making her forget he was four years her junior. His mere presence bolstered her confidence in a way that helped her believe she could accomplish anything. An image of a younger version of Walter demanding he escort her when he discovered she planned to secretly meet George in the gray early morning light flashed behind her closed eyelids. In an odd way, it had been Walter standing guard that had given her the courage to elope and marry George. The notion had her pressing her face further into the pillow.

Marrying George had meant she escaped the scrutinizing eyes of matrons who each season determined a lady's success or failure on the marriage mart. Her elopement also introduced her into a world of clandestine investigations and mysteries. Together, she and George had assisted in monitoring the activities of gentry and of the Network to ensure the preservation of the secret of PORFs' existence. George had given her access to a life she never could have imagined for herself. But last night she realized the effect Walter had upon her heart and soul—with him she was whole, not lacking in any manner. Walter's selflessness was pure. His love was unconditional.

Suffocating, Henrietta pushed the pillow aside and rolled over to her side. She skimmed her palm over the empty section of the bed—the space George had occupied throughout their marriage. Eyes closed, she pictured George, his lips always on tilt, ready with a quip to make her smile. A week prior to his death, he had cupped her cheek, and with seriousness he'd only displayed once before when he asked for her hand, the blasted man told her that she was still young and as a widow she should take full advantage of the liberties she was allowed as such.

Until now, she'd not given a second thought to George's words. Preoccupied with raising their boys, there was no time for flirting or liaisons. She ran her hand over her tender nipples that Walter had grazed with his teeth over and over. The glorious physical sensations Walter had evoked, ones she hadn't experienced in years, were nothing compared to the empowerment he unleashed within her. George had wanted her to be happy. Walter was a good man, a man George trusted with secrets he shouldn't have shared.

None of that changed the fact that Walter was four years her junior and sought after by others, including her close friend Bertha.

CHAPTER THIRTEEN

*P*acing, hands firmly clenched behind his back in front of George's gravesite, Walter muttered, "Why did you make me promise?"

He wanted to rail at the dead man. George had known how much Walter cared for Henrietta. The man had even proposed the preposterous idea of Walter joining them in the sanctity of their bedroom when Walter had come of age. When Walter had laughed at the suggestion, George had smiled and never made mention of it again. He knew George to be a free thinker, but Walter would never touch another man's wife—at least as long as the man was alive. Oh, he was no innocent. He was fully aware that couples engaged in many and varied activities. The truth was, he was selfish. He wanted Henrietta all to himself. The memory of Henrietta coming undone as he laved at her core stalled his movements.

Walter stood there staring at the tombstone of his

dearest secret friend. "Why did you not caution me of the dangers? Of the mystifying emotions that would ensue?"

Last night he had been imminently close to having his dreams of holding the woman his heart ached for all these years in his arms, but the ghost of a dead man had come between them once more. "I've tried to honor your memory and fulfill my promise to make her happy. But I'm at a loss as to how I can best satisfy everyone's wants—including my own. George. Forgive me."

The crunch of leaves halted his rant. Walter swung around to see who was approaching. The same lady in disguise as the local flower girl. She wore the same clean gray dress that peeked from beneath a great coat as she marched towards him.

Head bent with her hood pulled down low to mask her features, she stopped a foot away. "Me lord." She dipped, not quite a curtsy and not quite balanced. "Pardon fer interruptin'."

"I suppose you've come to claim the blunt I owe you." He reached into his coat pocket and pulled out a crown and rolled it between his fingers. "Except you don't need it, do you, my lady?"

The woman rolled back onto her heels. "Sumfin' wrong with yer eyes, me lord?"

"I think not." He took a step toward her and she mirrored his forward movement backward.

Upon a huff, she pushed back her hood.

"Lady Archbroke!"

"Pfft. Don't act surprised. You are the first and only to

have questioned me to date. Pray tell, what was it that led you to question my identity?"

"Lorna has been selling me flowers for years. While you mimicked her tone and cant extremely well, your soft skin and lack of grime under your nails and upon your skirts were clues to your real identity."

"My thanks. I shall have to endeavor to remember those items for the future."

"You think Lord Archbroke will continue to endorse such behavior after you begin to fill your nursery?"

"He's none the wiser at present, and I wish for that to continue. Landon assured me should you discover my identity I could trust you keep it a secret that I've yet to cease partaking in the occasional undercover activity."

"You are a Neale. I'd expect no less from you." He offered his arm, and she looped hers through his. "Why are you here today?"

"Landon suggested you might care for some company. Insinuated you had a complex matter that I might be able to assist with."

"Is that so?"

Theo puffed out her chest. "I've been told I'm rather good at devising schemes and finding solutions."

"Have you deciphered the key to love?"

She scanned the surroundings. "We shall need to relocate to somewhere more private for such discussions." She wagged her brow at him. "Nothing to fear, Lord Weathersbee, I'm well aware your heart and attentions belong only to one woman—my dear Aunt Henri."

"Have I made it that obvious?"

"Not at all." She maneuvered them to stroll along the perimeter headed toward the back gate where a non-descript coach was waiting. She paused by the gate. "You see, I'm quite observant and have the added benefit of wide and varied sources."

Mute, he held open the gate for Theo. He rolled his eyes heavenward. Theo was a PORF and had an entire Network of informants at her disposal. There was no telling what information she'd managed to obtain.

Waiting by the coach steps, Theo looked over her shoulder. "Will you be joining me or not?"

He slid the iron latch into place and turned to vault up into the coach. Seated on the rear-facing seat he said, "Lady Archbroke..."

"Please, call me Theo." She tapped the heel of her foot twice and the coach rolled into motion.

"Very well—Theo, why did Hadfield send you?" He jutted out his chin and continued, "And why did you opt to come in disguise?"

"Landon is a man of few words, but especially so when it comes to his mama's... personal affairs. He determined it best if I handle the situation, and I agreed."

"And as to you arriving in costume?"

She ran a hand over her gray ensemble and smiled. "Purely for my own benefit."

Theo was a delight to converse with normally but even more so when she let her guard down, which had never been the case before. "Do tell—what is it that you and Landon believe is the issue I need assistance with?"

"It is always difficult to know for certain what goes on

in my cousin's head; however, I'm fairly certain I'm correct that you are struggling to reconcile the depths of your affection for Aunt Henri and your loyalty to a dead man."

"I believe you are speaking to the wrong party. It is your aunt who is struggling with her attraction to me verses her wish to remain faithful to George. I've had several years of practice..."

Theo interrupted him exclaiming, "Balderdash! If that were the truth, why were you milling about and talking to a dead man?"

He took a moment to consider whether or not he should remain silent and let Theo come to her own conclusions, but the determined set of her features told him she'd patiently wait for his response. "For the majority of my life, Henrietta has been unattainable for one reason or another. To have held her in my arms and not merely in my dreams is rather disconcerting."

She pulled back the coach curtain briefly and peered out before returning her attention to him. "Did reality not live up to your fantasies or did the experience exceed your expectations?"

Having Henrietta come undone before him had been magnificent. This conversation was terribly uncomfortable, yet Theo's features were set with resolve and sympathy.

She leaned back against the coach squabs and rubbed her protruding stomach. "I fully understand how unusual this is, but I would strongly encourage you to allow me to assist."

Walter nodded and waited for Theo to continue.

"I know what it is like to sit on the fringes and observe a life you wish was yours. I watched and aided Lucy, Lady Devonton, for years in her role as the Home Office's primary decoder. I admit there were times when I was insanely jealous, but my love for her meant I only wished the best for her. I would never want to deny another their happiness." She let out a deep sigh. "After my papa made the extraordinary decision to leave to me responsibilities that rightfully Landon should have assumed and now does, my perspective on what I thought I'd always wanted and the reality of it were..."

Walter finished her thought. "Were vastly confusing. Exhilarating yet frightening."

"Frightening only because it was more than I'd hoped. My fear of loss and rejection was paralyzing. It resulted in me nearly losing the man I love dearly. I hope it doesn't do the same for you."

Walter stared at the young but exceptionally wise woman before him. "I shall endeavor to heed your advice."

"Wonderful. I shall drop you off in town. I have a suspicion my aunt will be in the mood for some sweet-meats today."

The woman was nothing if not strategic in her timing as the coach rolled to a stop a few yards away from Gunter's tea shop. With the coach door open, Walter shifted to leave. "I would like for you to become better acquainted with my nephew."

Theo had a playful smile upon her lips "Pfft. Lord

Darlington has more important matters to attend to than tea with the likes of me. However, I do wish him the best in his search for a marchioness."

"I shall convey your wishes to him." Walter dipped his head and then stepped down to the street.

"Please do." Theo's voice was strained, and she huffed a short breath. Mere moments before the footman closed the coach door, her features contorted, one eye half closed and the other squinted into a pained wink.

Walter stood mulling over Henrietta's mysterious niece. The lady had provided much to ponder. He didn't fear rejection; Henrietta's willing and enthusiastic responses to his touch had allayed any anxiety he may have had in that regard. However, he did fear the loss of two friendships he valued highly: those of a dead man and his wife.

CHAPTER FOURTEEN

*W*alter squinted in the direction of the tea shop and shook his head. The afternoon sun glinted off the shop windows to his left and caught his attention. Collins Confectionary. It wasn't the favored location by the ton, but Collins was the only vendor of salted chocolate-coated nuts—Henrietta's favorite. She would pop a sweetmeat in her mouth and close her eyes until all that remained was the nut.

He chuckled as he pushed the shop door open. Here he had thought Theo clever allowing him to disembark a discreet distance away from Gunter's, when in fact, the lady had placed him right in front of the shop front where he needed to be. He had underestimated Theo, and he certainly wouldn't make that mistake again.

"Hallo, Lord Weathersbee. Been a long time since ye've shown yer mug around these parts. Wot can I get ye today? Peppermints?"

"Not today. I'm here..."

Lady Bertha's excited voice from behind him stalled the rest of his sentence. The skin on the back of his neck rubbed against his cravat that suddenly felt too tight. Twisted at the waist, he beheld Henrietta, who stood with the sunlight glinting off the silver ribbon threaded through her pretty and very practical bonnet. Relief. Joy. Concern. All poured through Walter at Henrietta's meek smile. There was no trace of the friendly smile that she normally greeted him with, nor there was a hint of uncertainty. Was she regretting the shift in their relationship?

Lady Bertha stepped forward and bobbed a curtsy, blocking his view of Henrietta. He turned fully to face the women, "Lady Bertha. Henrietta." He tipped his head and bowed.

"Lord Weathersbee, what a delightful happenstance that you are here." Lady Bertha was glowing, considering her brush with scandal. It didn't appear she was suffering any ill effects of the abrupt ending of her courtship with Otterman. No signs of heartbreak or any other malady. She was obviously a very resilient woman.

"Quite a coincidence."

The two women shared a glance that held some meaning that he was attempting to decipher when Lady Bertha linked her arm about his and stepped forward, giving him no choice but to follow. Ushering him to the far corner of the store, Lady Bertha lowered her voice to a whisper, "I prefer the sweetmeats at Gunter's, but I understand for purposes of discretion why we must meet here."

Blimey. He hadn't orchestrated a meeting. Walter

glanced about, searching for Henrietta, but the woman wasn't in sight. Returning his attention back to Lady Bertha, he received sweet smile. Good lord, Lady Bertha was flirting with him.

Gently extracting his arm, Walter took a step back. "I beg your pardon, my lady, but I must set matters straight. I had no knowledge you would be frequenting this establishment."

"Then why are you here?" Lady Bertha's question was laced with disappointment.

Walter glanced around for the shopkeeper, hoping he could be extricated from this ridiculous situation. "I ventured in to purchase a bag of peppermints."

Mr. Collins appeared, brows knitted in confusion. "But me lord, ye said..."

Henrietta appeared out from the aisle next to them, causing Lady Bertha to take a small step back. Henrietta's warm, friendly smile had his heart doing somersaults in his chest. She turned to face the shopkeeper. "Ah, Mr. Collins, do you happen to have any of those chestnuts coated in chocolate and salt? They were most delicious."

"Oh, me eyes must be deceiving me. Is it really ye, Lady Henrietta? Ye haven't aged a day."

"You are too kind, sir. My papa disowned me long ago; I've not been a lady in sometime. However, I've led a very happy existence as Mrs. Neale."

It wasn't a lie. George had successfully seen to her happiness and since his departure, she appeared to have rejoiced in leading a life of independence. Walter's stomach began to churn. What could he bring to Henrietta's life that she needed?

"Ye will always be lady, ma'am. Now let me get ye a bag of them chocolates yer wantin'." Mr. Collins grinned, revealing a few missing teeth. Most likely the result of testing his wares.

Hiding behind Henrietta, Lady Bertha said, "I shall wait for you in the carriage." The woman scurried out of the store so fast, Henrietta hadn't managed to utter a reply.

Narrowing his gaze, he asked, "Why did Lady Bertha believe I had arranged for a surreptitious meeting?"

"She requested I inquire as to whether you..." Henrietta's eyes darted about, no doubt hoping Mr. Collins would appear and save her. Thankfully the shopkeep did not return with her sweetmeats.

"Henrietta?"

"She thinks of you as her knight, her savior. You did rescue her from Otterman. She is rather hopeful that perhaps you might have an interest in... her... to marry."

Walter inhaled sharply. "Marry Lady Bertha?" His roiling stomach clenched. Allowing Lady Bertha to believe that there was even a remote possibility he might entertain such a union was unlike Henrietta, unless she had decided not to further investigate which direction their relationship might take.

She placed a forefinger over his lips. "Shh."

Backing away from her touch, Walter replied, "Madam, don't shoosh me. I thought I'd made it quite clear who holds my interest."

RACHEL ANN SMITH

"I'm sorry." Henrietta had the sense to look abashed. She continued, "I... I simply haven't had the heart to inform Bertha."

He couldn't believe his ears. The Henrietta he grew up with never swayed away from difficult topics. The woman he knew had a keen ability to deliver the harshest of news with a skill that left the receiver unperturbed.

"You had best find the courage to do so and soon. Or would you prefer I take care of the matter?" Walter had never taken such a stern tone with her before. The bitter taste of betrayal upon his tongue gave his words an edge he rarely utilized.

Henrietta shook her head. "No. I shall convey the message. However, I'd prefer to do so while presenting her with alternative solutions."

Walter spied the glint in Henrietta's gaze that always appeared prior to her making some outlandish request. He held his breath and waited.

"I need some time. Would you be agreeable to a fortnight?"

Henrietta had lost her senses. If anyone knew how hurtful unrequited love could be, it was him. He didn't want to mislead Lady Bertha, but he was weak to Henrietta's pleading gaze. "A week, Henrietta and not a day longer."

The brilliant smile he received was indeed the best payment for his acquiescence.

After quickly checking to see no one was about, Henrietta leaned in and pressed her moist, plump lips to his. Before he could react, she pulled back and said, "My thanks, Walter. You won't regret agreeing, I promise."

The shuffle of footsteps behind her alerted the return of Mr. Collins. Henrietta turned to meet the shop-keep. He held out a palm-sized parcel tied with string. "Shall I be putting it on his account, like we used to?"

"Not this time, Mr. Collins. My son, Landon Neale, Lord Hadfield will settle my account."

Poor Mr. Collins's brow creased once more. "Yer son's Lord Hadfield?"

"Aye, he is."

"Then there's no account in need of settling." Mr. Collins bowed low as if he were addressing the queen.

Henrietta raised the package in the air and said, "My thanks to you, Mr. Collins. I shall make mention of your generosity to Landon this very eve."

Mr. Collin's cheeks burned red. "I appreciate it, me lady."

"Now, we've already been over this, Mr. Collins. I'm no longer a lady."

"Beggin' yer pardon, but ye'll always be a lady, no mind wot others may say."

Mr. Collins was right. Henrietta was a lady through and through. Ducal blood ran through her veins and she conducted herself in such a manner. No matter what her marital status deemed or if disowned by her own family, Henrietta was a lady.

Walter remained rooted to the spot until the shop door closed behind Henrietta.

Mr. Collins held out another wrapped package out for him. "Peppermints fer ye, Lord Weathersbee."

"My thanks, Mr. Collins." He took the package and slipped it into his coat pocket.

"Will ye be needin' anythin' else, me lord?"

Walter shook his head. "Nay, Mr. Collins. Not today."

The shop-keep nodded his head to the carriage moving into the traffic. "Ye'd be a fool to let that woman slip away from ye again."

"I don't intend to make the same mistakes as I did in my youth. However, she's recently returned to the bosom of the ton, and I'd prefer that I not be the reason she is once again ostracized."

Walter tipped his head as a farewell, leaving a stunned Mr. Collins behind as he exited the shop. Stepping out to hail a hack, the reality of his words hit hard, stealing his breath. He wanted to be able to love Henrietta openly, to finally act upon his desires. He no longer wished to censor his actions, but to do so would place her hard-won good standing amongst the ton in jeopardy.

CHAPTER FIFTEEN

*T*he footman patiently held open the coach door for Henrietta. She wasn't one to take mincing steps, but she needed an extra moment to settle the fluttering in her chest stemming from uncertainty of the best approach with which to handle the discussion about to ensue with Bertha. Henrietta ducked her head as she entered the vehicle, settled upon the forward-facing seat, and took in a fortifying breath as she busied herself with adjusting her skirts. Avoiding her friend's scrutiny, she let her eyes roam over the intricate floral design of the interior fabric next to Bertha's shoulder. The click-clack of the horses' hooves upon the cobblestone street was the only sound that filled the air. Their carriage came to a halt once more in the afternoon crush.

Henrietta swallowed the lump in her throat. Her heart ached with knowing she should say something. "Bertha, I'm sorry..."

Bertha raised a gloved hand in the air. "Don't apologize; I shouldn't have assumed you had already spoken to Lord Weathersbee." Her hand fell back to her lap, but her gaze never wavered. "You remained in Mr. Collins's shop a fair while. Were you able to find out if there was a possibility Lord Weathersbee might hold a tendre for me?"

"Weathersbee is a renowned bachelor. It's doubtful he'll ever marry." The statement, while true, left Henrietta's chest aching for the man. Never married, Walter would never know the bond formed between husband and wife. While she may hesitate to express her true feelings for the man, a second marriage was not what Henrietta envisioned for her future. She relished her legal and financial independence too much to relinquish it.

"How will I ever weather the scandal of a broken engagement?" Bertha buried her face in her hands. "Lady Marion and the others will surely give me the cut direct. Their favor is as fickle as the wind." She shook her head. "What good is the old drafty home I inherited if I'm to sit in it all alone?"

The ache in Henrietta's chest deepened at the sight of her friend's distress. Bertha deserved better. She didn't have a mean bone in her body, unlike the male members of her family. It was Bertha's brother Bartholomew's fault for the lack of offers for Bertha's hand. He was a tyrant. Henrietta despised men that abused their position in life. Bertha had written to Henrietta over the years detailing Bartholomew's treachery and schemes to use her to improve his situation—vying for votes in the House of Lords from potential suitors and bargaining her dowry for favors. As the years passed, Henrietta learned of Bertha's plight as she was relegated to the fringes. Meanwhile, Henrietta had been safe under George's protection and given opportunities to grow and blossom as a PORF. Henrietta didn't fault Bertha for leaping at the chance to escape her brother now that she had inherited a small fortune from a distant aunt who had cleverly devised the bequest to ensure Bartholomew couldn't access the funds. No, it was Bertha's chance, and she was going to help her friend.

Henrietta leaned forward and pulled Bertha's hands away from her tear-streaked face. "Do you trust me?"

"Aye. I should have heeded your warnings regarding Lord Otterman from the beginning."

"Let's not rehash that matter." Henrietta released Bertha and sat back, tapping her forefinger against her chin. "Tell me, are there any other gentlemen of your acquaintance besides Weathersbee that you might be fond of?"

Bertha's features brightened. Bertha wasn't one to wallow in pity. It was a quality Henrietta treasured about her friend. "Well, I quite enjoy conversing with Lord Morseworth and Mr. Grandshaw, but both gentlemen are younger than I."

"You had no objections to Weathersbee and he is your junior by two years, is he not?"

"Yes, but Weathersbee...Weathersbee is, well, the exception. He would be worth the risk of ostracization." Bertha's dreamy gaze vanished as she gave her head a shake. "I shall need to think upon it more."

While Bertha pondered, Henrietta's heart raced. Walter was four years her junior. Having been disowned, Henrietta existed on the outer fringes of beau monde for years. It would be no hardship for her to live in the shadows once again, but could Walter?

Bertha exhaled deeply before saying, "Lord Bartram recently lost his wife, but he's in mourning."

"But we both know the rules of mourning are never observed by men."

Bertha's eyes lit up. "Lord Bartram also has two lovely children." Her friend would make for a wonderful mama. Bartram's name didn't raise any alarm bells in Henrietta's mind, and she couldn't recall any recent gossip, good or bad, involving the man, but the skin on the back of her neck prickled. She'd have to make inquiries.

"Will you assist me in gaining Lord Bartram's attention? I need to wed if Marina is to remain untainted by my hash of an engagement."

Typical of Bertha, her motivation wasn't out of selfishness to escape her awful brother, it was to help her young cousin. Henrietta bemoaned, "I'd forgotten how difficult it is navigating the whims of the ton."

Bertha beamed a smile at her. "Yet you have managed to these two years past with ease."

"Ease!"

"Very well, with grace."

Bertha really was a magnificent, loyal friend. Henrietta returned Bertha's smile. "I couldn't have done it without you and your support. As repayment I shall endeavor to find you a suitable husband within the week."

Reaching for both of Henrietta's hands and giving them a squeeze, Bertha said, "You are the very best of friends. I shall forever be in your debt."

A large lump formed in Henrietta's throat. "No, it is I who shall always be indebted to you." If Henrietta failed to succeed in making a match for Bertha, then there was no hope of maintaining the woman's friendship, especially once Henrietta revealed her true feelings for Walter.

Thankfully the momentum of the coach was slowing. Bertha released Henrietta's hands and gave her a wide smile as she prepared to exit. "Thank you, Henrietta. You have no idea how wonderful it will be to be free of my family."

Henrietta returned Bertha's smile and waited for her friend to descend before expelling the breath she was holding. Bertha was wrong, Henrietta knew all too well how liberating it was to be distanced from one's own archaic, male-dominated blood relations, but it was also a painful burden to know you would never be accepted by them either.

CHAPTER SIXTEEN

*S*lumped in the corner of the coach, Henrietta was thankful for their plodding pace for the first time in a long time. Events and conversations of the past week were testing her resilience. Emotions she normally kept tightly sealed away kept threating to erupt. There was no one about to see her crying, and so she allowed the singular tear to escape the corner of her eye and roll down her cheek.

Devoting her time to others had allowed her to avoid dealing with the reality that she was all alone. Her papa's disownment had been bittersweet, for she gave up her position in a ducal family that, as hard as it was to admit, never really loved her, to marry into the Hadfield family, who wholeheartedly loved and embraced her. Older and wiser, she acknowledged her youthful need to prove herself and become an essential member of the PORFs had been to ensure she would never give another family a reason to renounce her. An intimate relationship with a man many years her junior would again have the tongues of the ton wagging. If she was to continue to assist Landon and remain useful as a PORF, it would not be wise to entertain such an entanglement. Bah. To hell with what the ton might say, but what would her children think of her?

The coach door flung open. Back at her son's townhouse. If she was quick about it, she might make it to her chambers without notice. Bronwyn appeared and entered, flopping into the seat next to her. Landon and Archbroke also joined them, occupying every inch of the rear-facing seat.

Henrietta noted Archbroke's strained features. "What in the blazes is going on?"

Both Bronwyn and Archbroke looked to Landon. "We are all adjourning to the Archbroke residence."

"Why?"

"Given my dear cousin's condition, I believed it wise." Landon crossed his arms over his chest and smiled. "I have also requested that Weathersbee invite Lady Irene to join us for the afternoon."

From the corner of her eye, Henrietta caught Bronwyn arching an eyebrow in Landon's direction. The two were silently conversing, neither willing to look away first. Normally, Henrietta would be highly entertained and a willing witness to a contest of wills between her son and daughter-in-law; however, she had an unnerving feeling that *she* was the topic of debate today.

Archbroke tugged on his mangled rose-pink silk

cravat. "Weathersbee had best be prompt. I've a few queries of my own for the man."

"What matters do you have to discuss with Walter?"

Archbroke's stare could intimidate his agents at the Home Office, but Henrietta was immune. The coach came to an abrupt stop. Her arms flew out wide to the sides to brace herself and hold Bronwyn back so she wouldn't fall to her knees, but her arm met the back of the seat cushion.

Landon had already hauled his wife protectively into his lap. He whispered, "I relent. I promise to remain open minded."

The coach door opened, and a distressed footman stuck his head in. "Apologies, my lord."

Extracting herself from Landon's arms, Bronwyn gave the footman a reassuring smile. "Not to worry, we are well."

Henrietta followed her grinning daughter-in-law out of the coach. Scanning her surroundings, she saw no obvious cause for the coachman to have brought the coach to such an abrupt halt.

Bronwyn hooked her arm through Henrietta's. "Let's not keep Theo waiting, Mama." In unison, they marched up the front steps to Archbroke's townhouse.

Ooh, Bronwyn was up to no good. "What are you scheming, *child*?"

Stalling in the front door threshold, Bronwyn pointed to her own chest and feigned indignation. "Me? Why would you believe I was..."

Henrietta chuckled. "Enough play acting. You are

terrible at it." Henrietta strode through the townhome, leading the way to Theo's private study.

A footman bowed. "Lady Henrietta. Countess Hadfield." He stepped forward, slowing her progress. "Lady Archbroke, Lord Weathersbee and Lady Irene are waiting in the blue drawing room."

The green drawing room was typically reserved for receiving visitors, not the blue. Bronwyn asked, "What is Theo thinking?"

"We won't know unless we make haste and join her." Henrietta swiveled in the direction of the drawing room that was designed to accommodate all three PORF families. With Bronwyn, Landon, and Archbroke following behind her, Henrietta walked briskly, clutching at her skirts so as not to trip over them. She spied Archbroke's stoic butler, Hinley, standing guard at the door. How peculiar.

Straightening to attention, Hinley nodded as he pushed open the door and promptly announced their arrival. Henrietta froze at the sight of Lady Irene rubbing Theo's back while Walter muttered and walked in a small, tight circle. Her niece bent at the waist, clutching the back of an oversized chaise lounge. They were on the opposite side of the massive drawing room, too far away to hear precisely what Walter was saying. Archbroke rushed past Henrietta to Theo's side, sending Walter and Lady Irene looks that might have turned them to stone had he been Medusa.

Theo straightened and adopted Henrietta's favored stance. Hands on her hips, Theo glared at her husband.

"Archbroke, that is no way to greet our guests." She turned to address Lady Irene. Her hands slipped to rest on the small of her back. "I shall endeavor to heed your advice when the time comes." Theo waddled around to settle herself against the back of the chaise lounge. "Now, that the rest of our party has arrived, I'd like to share my thoughts on how best to proceed in order to resolve *your* predicament."

Archbroke immediately took his position behind Theo. Henrietta moved to sit upon the settee opposite Theo, followed by Bronwyn. Landon made his way to stand next to Walter, who had managed to place two pieces of furniture between himself and Archbroke. Everyone moved like orchestrated chess pieces except for Lady Irene.

Bronwyn scooted closer to Henrietta. "Lady Irene, please come join us."

Once Lady Irene was settled, Theo said, "Based on the information Lord Weathersbee has shared with me —" Theo glanced over her shoulder at her husband. "That is, prior to our interruption, I surmise it imperative you marry Lord Otterman without delay." Theo shifted her gaze to Bronwyn.

The pause was no longer than three heartbeats before Bronwyn said, "Lord Hadfield and I will be more than happy to act as witnesses and assist with the arrangements."

Lady Irene tilted her head in Bronwyn's direction. "My thanks for your support, but why are you assisting

Charlie and me? I'm a stranger to you. My own family wishes to have nothing to do with me."

Henrietta sensed a wave of heat about her. She turned. Walter's eyes were trained upon her. He was concerned for her. She would be a liar if she said she remained unaffected by Lady Irene's words. After all these years, she had become numb to the hurt of her family's continued stance to denounce her even when Landon ascended in title. But the comfort of having Walter close by was new.

Bronwyn's proud, confident voice broke through her thoughts. "The answer is simple: because my cousin, Theo, is an extremely good judge of character. And the moment I saw you easing Theo's pain with long methodical strokes, I knew you were a kind caring soul."

"You summarized all that in mere moments?" Lady Irene asked.

Landon answered before his wife could, "We all did. Including Archbroke. He gets extremely jealous when he sees another touching his wife, regardless if they are male or female." Landon winked in Archbroke's direction, which garnered chuckles from everyone.

Henrietta caught Theo yawning, and so did Landon and Walter. If Theo was in early labor as Henrietta suspected, it would be best if Theo rested before the baby decided to join them. She gave her son the barest of nods, and both men were set into motion.

Walter casually walked over to stand beside Henrietta, and Landon to stand before Bronwyn. "Wife, Lady

Irene, we should take our leave. There is much to accomplish."

Bronwyn and Lady Irene both stood to depart.

Lady Irene took two steps, but then whirled around to bend over and whisper in Theo's ear. Theo's eyes went wide, and she shifted her gaze to Archbroke and then back to Lady Irene again. The girl shrugged her shoulders and said for all to hear, "The midwife swears it works every time."

Flanked by Bronwyn and Lady Irene, Landon escorted the ladies from the room.

Theo's gaze locked on Henrietta. Henrietta rummaged through the slew of birthing advise her own midwife had provided. She wanted to roll her eyes as she recalled her midwife laughing and saying, "Marital relations is wot got ye here, and it might well be the answer to getting the bub out." Henrietta gave Theo a wink and a nod.

"I believe I've had enough excitement today." Theo rolled to her feet. "Dear, will you escort me to our chambers?"

Walter glanced down at Henrietta and mouthed—is all well? Henrietta gave him a broad smile and nodded.

Archbroke scooped his very pregnant wife up into his arms and cradled her to him. "It would be my pleasure, love."

Looking over her husband's shoulder, Theo grinned and said, "Lord Weathersbee, please stay. I'm certain Aunt Henri will be able to assist you with the last few remaining items to be resolved."

Henrietta burst into laughter as soon as the door clicked closed.

"What is so amusing?" Walter asked.

WALTER'S LIPS curved into a smile as he admired Henrietta's merriment. He always believed her beautiful, but with her cheeks flushed, her eyes twinkling with glee, and lips slightly parted, Henrietta was stunning to behold.

She clutched her stomach and inhaled deeply. "Archbroke has no idea what Theo has planned for him, and it is supremely satisfying to see my niece keep her genius of a husband on his toes."

"Why do you not whole heartedly approve of Archbroke? He appears to be a devoted husband, and unquestionably in love with Theo."

"Mayhap it is because I'm a tad protective of Theo. Having lost all the members of her immediate family, I never want her to feel alone."

Henrietta's answer was revealing. Embraced as she had been by George and his family, Walter never considered the impact upon Henrietta of having been isolated from her family. Her ducal family were a dull lot, whereas Henrietta was a perfect fit within the Hadfields.

He moved to sit upon the settee next to Henrietta. "Did you feel alone after your papa disowned you?"

She shifted closer and he wrapped his arm about her shoulders. The need to protect her from hurt manifested within him in a way it never had before. He could easily guard her from an outside physical threat, but to safeguard her heart would require more consideration.

Faced away from him, she answered, "There were times when I wished to have my mama's counsel. However, Theo's grandmama always sensed those moments and provided me reassurance and advice that I've come to realize my own mama was incapable of providing. My hope is that I can continue to be here for Theo, like her grandmama was for me." She shifted and placed her palm over his chest. "Enough about me. What are we to do about Otterman and Lady Irene?"

"Otterman's finances are a fine mess but not as dismal as he believes. He simply needs to be taught how to balance his estate ledgers correctly." He liked the feel of her hand on him, but it was also greatly distracting.

Henrietta patted him over his heart. "Are you to be Otterman's tutor?" She ran her finger down the seam of his jacket, freeing one button at a time.

"Actually, I've assigned the task to Nicholas. He has a fine mind for numbers and a deeper well of patience than I possess. Did you manage to sort matters with Bertha?"

She slipped her hand under the material of his jacket. "Aye. We discussed a number of other eligible men, and I believe she now has her sights on one of them."

He pulled her closer and dipped his head for a quick kiss. The pretty pink blush reappeared on her cheeks.

"Speaking of your nephew, has he mentioned who will be his marchioness?"

"No. However, he has denounced the idea of a love match."

"How interesting." She wrapped both arms about his waist and pressed her cheek to him. "We shall have to join forces and see that he accepts every invitation that hits your salver."

Hugging her to him, he basked in the idea of partnering with Henrietta. Before his mind could stray, Walter released a groan and said, "There are matters I must attend to at the office."

She pulled back and smiled. "I understand." Henrietta stood and held out her hand for him.

He took her hand and brought it to his lips before standing. He was a fool to forgo this opportunity, but they were in Archbroke's home and he had delayed attending to his duties at Neale & Sons too many hours already. Henrietta led him out to the foyer and he collected his hat, gloves, and great coat from Hinley, who discreetly backed away.

Rolling to her tiptoes, Henrietta placed a chaste kiss upon his cheek. "I look forward to seeing you later this eve." She turned him about and gently pushed him towards the door.

He opened the door to exit but at the last moment glanced over his shoulder to watch Henrietta disappear down the hallway. He bounded down the steps, attempting to recall what event he was to attend later that eve. He rubbed his temple. He had no recollection of accepting any invitations for that evening. The woman was clearly up to something.

CHAPTER SEVENTEEN

*B*lurry eyed after spending hours reviewing files and catching up on the administration of Neale & Sons, Walter marched up the steps of Lord Archbroke's townhouse for the second time that day. Why the Home Office Secretary had summoned him was beyond his tired mind and empty stomach. When he'd left earlier, Walter had been under the belief all was well. He reached up for the knocker, but before he even had his arm raised shoulder level, the front door swung open.

A disheveled looking butler appeared in the entrance. "Lord Weathersbee. Please follow me."

Lord Archbroke's growls echoed through the house. "What the bloody hell..."

Halting before a door, the butler inhaled deeply and squared his shoulders. "Ready, my lord?"

What a peculiar question. Stiffening his spine, Walter nodded.

The door swung open to reveal the lavish blue

drawing room full of members from both the Archbroke and Hadfield families.

The butler cleared his throat and announced, "Lord Weathersbee."

Walter faced the inquiring eyes and took a step forward. He turned back around as the whoosh of air hit the back of his neck. The door closed, eliminating a quick escape.

Henrietta approached like an angel sent to save him. "Walter, please come join us."

He lowered his voice to a whisper. "Why have I been summoned?"

"Theo requested your presence." Henrietta led him to the settee where her niece sat calmly with one hand gently resting over her protruding stomach and her other arm wrapped about a small girl snuggled to her side.

Surrounded by the Hadfields, who were severely outnumbered by members of the Archbroke family, Walter bowed. "At your service, Lady Archbroke."

Giving the little girl one last squeeze before removing her arm, Theo said, "Why don't you go join your mama."

"Yes, Aunt Theo." Obediently the girl slid to her feet and scurried over to join her family.

Theo shifted and patted the velvet cushioned seat. "Please, come sit."

Well aware that every set of eyes were upon him, Walter sat, careful not to crowd the woman. A large, dark shadow fell over Theo. Both her husband and cousin now stood behind her. He had a newfound respect for those debutantes who had paraded before the queen and now fully understood why Henrietta had been willing to do anything to avoid her coming out.

Swallowing the lump in his throat, he waited for Theo, whose eyes were closed tight. He leaned in closer so only she could hear. "Are you all right, Theo?"

Nodding, she moved her hands and placed them behind her, kneading her lower back. "Lord Weathersbee, it has come to my attention that my dear departed uncle entrusted you with information that, for generations, has been privy to only those who were either born or married into the entrusted families that have sworn secret oaths to Protect the Royal Family." She glanced up at her cousin, Landon, who according to Walter's sources was the Head PORF, before continuing, "We wish for you to explain the extent of your knowledge."

"I have a few questions of my own that I'd like answered before I fulfill your request."

Theo laughed. "Ah... yes, you are a keen negotiator after all. But unfortunately, in this instance your inquiries will have to wait. Please—share with us what you know of our organization."

Surrounded, he didn't have much choice. "George imparted to me the names of the trinity of families deemed PORFs, their responsibilities, and described the symbol each of you bear. He also described the symbol identifying those who have sworn a fealty to serve PORFs, your Network."

"Bloody Neale family," Archbroke cursed.

Landon gave Theo's husband a cutting look, prompting a quick apology from the man.

Ignoring the men behind her, Theo captured Walter's attention by leaning forward and grasping his hand that was tightly clenched over his knee. "Lord Weathersbee, I must ask, have you shared any of this information with another?"

"No! George made it quite clear that should I tell anyone, it would place them in imminent danger."

"Not even your nephew, Lord Darlington?"

Walter flinched at the implication he'd place his nephew in harm's way. "Most certainly not."

"And you have kept this secret for decades?"

"Aye."

Theo released her hold on his wrist and twisted to address her cousin. "I believe him."

Archbroke smiled at his wife and turned to address Landon. "I concur."

Unlike Theo and Archbroke's quick declarations, Landon's assessing gaze remained upon him. His breath caught in his chest as he waited for Landon's decision as Head PORF. Walter did not envy the boy—to segregate his emotions and roles must be extremely difficult. He wanted Landon's approval but more as Henrietta's son than as Head PORF. Perhaps in this instance, the man's approval was one and the same. Finally, Landon gave the briefest of nods, spurring the Archbroke family into motion. Like a hive of bees, they fell into formation and headed for the door. Amid the chaos, Theo grabbed Walter's arm. "Lord Weathersbee, I need your assistance." The woman was going to leave a bruise, she was squeezing his arm so hard.

He asked, "What is it you need?"

"I need you to tell Landon to take his wife home immediately, have my aunt assist me to my rooms and you..." She shut her eyes and pressed her lips together tight. "And you... you must distract Archbroke until I send for him. Do you understand?"

Walter nodded. Theo was obviously in discomfort and she wanted her succinct orders to be executed immediately.

He rose, made haste to Henrietta's side and bent to whisper. "Theo needs you, now."

Henrietta calmly took his proffered hand and rose. "Archbroke will be a bear, but you must keep him company until it is time."

"I shall do my best."

Henrietta smiled and placed a chaste kiss upon his cheek. A burst of joy hit him at the realization she had dared to show him affection in front of her family. Granted they were all bound to secrecy, but he dared not think what it all meant this moment.

Walter moved to speak to the men huddled in deep discussion.

Bronwyn reached him first. "What is the matter? Why did my mother-in-law just give me the most peculiar look?"

Altering Theo's request to his advantage, he replied, "Theo has asked you take your husband home." He'd much prefer to deal with the countess than attempt to order Henrietta's son about.

In true Neale fashion, Countess Hadfield questioned, "Why?"

"My guess is that Theo does not wish to subject you to her screams. Although, she doesn't strike me as the sort to yell no matter the provocation."

Acknowledgment registered on the countess's features. "Are you to remain and deal with Archbroke?"

"Aye."

She gave her head a slight shake and then smiled. "You are a brave soul."

Walter followed Bronwyn as she made her way to Landon's side.

"Husband, perhaps you could allow Archbroke to explain everything to Lord Weathersbee."

Landon peered down at his wife.

The curl of Bronwyn's lips, and the devilish wink she hid from Archbroke, had Landon bidding them a hasty goodbye and ushering Bronwyn out of the room.

Archbroke glanced about and narrowed his eyes. "What the devil is going on, Weathersbee?"

"I'm to keep you company until..."

"Until my wife summons me." He walked over to the sideboard and poured drinks for them both. "Why I ever agreed to remain in town, I shall never know."

Walter took the glass full with liquor. "It's extremely difficult to say no to a Neale woman."

Archbroke laughed. "Weathersbee, I understand why Theo's uncle trusted you. You are an extremely astute gentleman and one with much courage."

"That, or I'm merely a fool in love."

Archbroke raised his glass in the air. "To fools in love."

His celebratory statement was punctuated by the first of Theo's screams. "'Tis all Archbroke's bloody fault!"

Archbroke gulped down the contents of his glass and set it upon the side table. "I'm sure she'll remember how much I love her... won't she?"

Walter shrugged. "Perhaps, but I suggest we remain here..."

"I should be with her." Archbroke marched to the door. "Theo's absolutely correct. Her agony is all my doing." He tugged on the door latch, but it did not budge. "Damn it, they've locked us in."

To watch the respected Home Secretary brought to his knees by a woman was eye opening. Having witnessed Archbroke and Theo's interactions at various social events, theirs was not an obvious love match. Yet as he watched Archbroke pace erratically about the room and deciphered the man's mutterings, it was clear that Archbroke's union with Theo was founded on love and trust. He had masked his feeling for Henrietta for years. Could he, like Archbroke, love unconditionally before family and refrain from exhibiting such feelings in the company of the ton?

CHAPTER EIGHTEEN

*S*weat dripped from Theo's temple. "Why would any woman subject herself to such pain multiple times?"

Henrietta rubbed her niece's back as they paced back and forth in front of the gargantuan bed in the chamber that traditionally was occupied by only the master of the house but was unconventionally shared by both Theo and her husband. "How long have you been experiencing pain?"

Theo stalled and wiped her brow with the washcloth that had been cool to the touch when Henrietta had given it to her before they began pacing. "Lucy said the birthing pains could begin days before my body is truly ready…"

"Your best friend was pregnant with twins. Lucy's situation was entirely different, and in fact no two births are the exact same." Henrietta took the damp cloth Theo was hiding behind and asked again, "When did they begin?"

"Well, it might have been when I was saying goodbye to Lord Weathersbee in front of Mr. Collins's shop."

"Good gracious, why did you not inform me earlier?"

"There was no need." Theo took a tentative step forward but halted to inhale deeply before continuing, "Lucy was rather descriptive of the signs I should watch for."

The midwife squeezed through the doorway, hauling with her a birthing chair. A line of maids followed; some had arms full of linens and others carried pails of water.

Theo padded over to lean against the bed. "Why the glare, Aunt Henri?"

She pulled back the bed linens. "You should allow your husband to be in here with you if he wishes to be."

"Was Uncle George present during the births of your boys?"

Henrietta smiled. "Aye. He was present in the creation of those children, and he was there when they joined us upon this earth. You know your uncle never thought much about traditions."

Rubbing the small of her back, Theo answered, "I am well aware, Aunt Henri, of how untraditional our family can be."

The midwife approached. "My lady, I need to examine ye to see how far along ye are. Please lie upon the bed for a moment."

Theo crawled up onto the bed. "I am a tad scared. Would you mind..." Theo paused.

Her niece was extremely proud. It was rare for Theo to admit to fear. Henrietta smiled and said, "I shall fetch your husband."

"Thank you, Aunt Henri. For everything."

Henrietta left the room, lifted her skirts, and ran as fast as she could down the stairs to the drawing room. She nodded to the poor footman standing guard. He removed the chair that was barricading the entrance and opened the door for her. Stiffening her spine and raising her chin, she marched in to face Archbroke. He was a wonderful, loving husband to Theo despite his natural overbearing tendency to take charge of every situation.

"Archbroke. It is time you joined Theo."

"Am I a papa already?"

"Not that I am aware. However, Theo needs..."

Archbroke was already racing out the door.

Wide eyed, Walter turned and said, "I should take my leave now."

"I'd prefer you stay and pour me a drink."

"Are you not going back to tend to Theo?"

"No, she has her husband and a very competent midwife." Henrietta sank into the settee Theo had occupied earlier. "Please stay and keep me company?"

Walter moved to the sideboard. "Madeira or something stronger?"

"Brandy. Seeing my stalwart niece in distress has me..."

Walter held out a glass containing a splash of deep amber liquid. "Upset. Reliving the experience?"

Taking the glass with two hands, she took a sip. "It's

odd. During the birthing of both my boys, I swore to never let George touch me again. But within weeks, the memories of the discomfort were muted and soon forgotten." She reached out and tugged on his hand.

Walter sat silently next to her.

"Did you not want children of your own?"

"No—not for a single moment. After all, when I became guardian to both my brothers' offspring, I had my hands full."

Henrietta raised her glass. "You have raised your charges to be well-respected members of society."

Their glasses clinked. "As have you." Walter finished the contents of his glass and shifted to place the glass upon the side table. There was weariness to his movements.

She waited for him to meet her gaze. "Is there something amiss?"

"Nay."

"Do you regret kissing me?"

"I remember this about you. Always questioning."

"Then you should recall that I'm not one easily dissuaded." She shifted closer. "What is the matter?"

He sighed. "I love you. I've loved you every moment since the day you found me lost in the woods."

She loved him too, but the words remained caught in her heart. She moved back to the furthest corner of the settee and gently positioned him to lean back and rest his head in her lap like they had long ago. "Do you remember when we would sit in the grass?"

Eyes closed, Walter remained tense. She ran her

finger over his brow and his features softened. "I remember everything."

She cupped his jaw and stroked his cheek with her thumb. "The fondest moments of my childhood are those when it was just the two of us."

He opened his eyes. "Those are mine as well." He placed a hand over hers, halting her movements. "I wished and prayed every night that things could remain the same, that we didn't have to grow up, that you would wait for me. But then I met George. He was the man I wanted to be when I matured. He loved you just as much as I. He was the perfect gentleman."

Henrietta chuckled, bobbing her head up and down. She trailed her hand down to his chest. "George was many things, but he was not perfect. And in a peculiar way, I did end up waiting for you." She released each button of his jacket. As she bent over him, his breath warmed the top of her breasts. She no longer wanted to reminisce over the past, she wanted to create fresh memories with Walter. Working on the buttons of his waistcoat, Henrietta gasped as Walter's hands pulled her down by the shoulders. The tip of his tongue slipped between the valley between her bosoms. Sliding her hands to his side, she tugged fiercely at his lawn shirt, freeing it from his breeches. She slipped her hand lower, under his waistband, to cup his engorged manhood. He was well endowed.

Panting, Walter said, "Henrietta. We must stop."

"Why?" She pulled her hand away and straightened.

"We are in Archbroke's home."

167

Recalling their location coupled with the realization that Theo's wailing had subsided, Henrietta said, "Ah. You are right, we should move to a more private location." She grabbed his hand and hauled him over to the secret passage.

"Where are you taking me?"

She stilled his hands, which were attempting to tuck the ends of his shirt back into place. She stepped closer and whispered, "To my chambers."

He tugged at his cravat that sat askew. "You have rooms here too?"

"Yes. It was all arranged weeks ago." She pulled on the lever to release the latch and pulled the secret door open. "All PORF residences are designed the same. Since you already know of most of our secrets, sharing this won't be any different." She tugged him into the tight passageway. Pressed up against him, she let the excitement settle before tugging the entrance closed. She waited a moment to let their eyes adjust to the darkness. Only small peep holes along the corridor allowed the barest of light in.

Tugging on his hand, she led him to her chambers. With each step her pulse increased from both excitement and apprehension.

CHAPTER NINETEEN

*S*tepping out of the dark, Walter released Henrietta's hand and blinked to clear his vision. He made his way to the fireplace and rested his forearm against the mantel. The fire was already ablaze, as were his insides after Henrietta's lush body rubbed against his multiple times during their trek to her chambers. He took deep, calming breaths as she pattered about the room. Henrietta's eager responses to his kisses earlier left him no doubt she was a willing participant, but lingering concerns over the possible ramifications had him second guessing his every action.

Henrietta's spacious receiving room was quiet. He peered about, but she was nowhere in sight. "Henrietta, dear, where are you?"

"I'm in my dressing chambers." Her voice came from another connecting room.

Walter ventured into the next room that was furnished with only a petite writing desk and chair. The back wall was lined with bookshelves and an impressive collection of volumes. Archbroke's residence appeared modest in size from the street front, but the house and the extended quarters were both more than adequately sized. Knowing of PORFs and their existence had been an easy secret to maintain from afar, but being amongst them and in close contact was entirely a different matter. Moving in the direction of Henrietta's voice, he entered her bedchambers. A maid scurried past, pretending not to notice his presence, and quietly left through the door to the main hallway.

Henrietta emerged garbed in a pretty pink silk dressing gown with a sash tied at the waist. "I see you found me." She marched up to him and took his hand in hers.

Leading him like she had when they were youths, Henrietta drew him closer to the bed. Her solid grip on him unraveled the nervous knots in his stomach. She hopped onto the bed and knelt before him. "May I?" She fiddled with a button at his falls.

Dry mouthed, all he could do was nod. Henrietta grinned and made quick work of assisting him to strip out of his clothes. He bent to slip his feet out of his breeches and discard his stockings. When he straightened, he found Henrietta sitting in the middle of the bed no longer wrapped in a robe. The thin material of her chemise stretched taut over her generous bosom sent all the blood in his body rushing below his navel.

"I shan't let you leave this time." Henrietta pulled

back the linens. "At least not until we have both found our pleasure."

He crawled up on to the bed and slid in next to her. "I found it both satisfying and fulfilling to see you come undone," Walter admitted.

She pressed her warm body closer. "Make no mistake, Walter Weathersbee, I *will* keep you abed until we are both fully sated." Henrietta's eyes momentarily dropped below his waistline. Eyes full of excitement returned to his own. "Even if it takes all night and all morn. Am I clear?"

"Aye, I fully understand your meaning."

Henrietta shifted, aligning her body with his and instantly smothering him. He was in heaven. Her eagerness had every cell in his body sparking to life. Some men might prefer a passive woman; however, Walter favored women who were bold and daring both in and out of the bed chamber. Henrietta didn't disappoint. She raked her fingernails through his hair and over his scalp as she took his lips in a searing and unrelenting kiss. Her tongue darted out and collided with his. Now, *this* was kissing and what he had waited so long for.

Gathering the material of her sheer nightgown at her hips, he rolled so they were both on their sides. Henrietta's kisses intoxicated him. He would be content to have her lips on his all eve, but her deep throated moans and the restlessness of her hips indicated she wanted more. His heart soared. Henrietta desired him.

Her hardened nipples pressed against his chest until

he was on his back once more. Willing to submit, Walter took pleasure at the heightened color of Henrietta's cheeks as she straddled him, her plump bottom pressing against his erect manhood. She ran her hands down his arms and brought his hands up to cup her delightfully full breasts. Heart racing, he rubbed his thumbs over her tender flesh. He was a quick study, and having learned from his previous attentions, he knew she was partial to both the feel of his tongue on the underside of her breasts and the light grazing of his fingernails along her sides. Her body responded to varying pressured touches rather than nipple stimulation. He wanted to learn every pleasure zone upon Henrietta's lush body. He would not be satisfied until he identified all her preferences. But tonight, it was obvious she was intent on learning his body. She pulled her shift over her head and haphazardly dropped it to the floor. Shimmying lower, Henrietta bent and aligned her lips over his right nipple. Her tongue darted over her lips as if she were about to experience a taste of her favorite treat. Walter rested his head back and closed his eyes. Her warm breath teased him first, then the tip of her tongue circled his hard nipple. A groan of pleasure escaped him before she flicked the sensitive bud and his hips bucked at the stimulation. He couldn't stand it a moment longer—he wanted her to ride him, but when he opened his eyes, she was trailing her lips across his chest.

Henrietta peered up through her lashes at him. "I fully submitted to your slow and methodical provocation the other eve without protest, and you shall grant me the same courtesy."

He'd never deny her a wish. He blinked twice, their old childhood code for yes. She pursed her lips and sent a light flow of air over his sensitive skin. The glint of happiness in Henrietta's gaze was irresistible. He'd succumb to her every wish and demand.

Done teasing his nipple, she began torturing him by skimming light kisses along his neck. His cock was hard and bumped against her soft ass. She straightened at the light tap, rose to her knees, and scooted back until she hovered over him. Taking him in her hand, she ran the tip of him along her wet, ready slit and then over the nub of flesh that he'd rubbed over and over with his thumb the other eve to bring her to ecstasy. The sensitive skin brushing over hers sent shock waves through him all the way to his curled toes.

Her hand tightly wrapped around his manhood as she leaned forward to whisper in his ear. "Ready?"

He blinked twice again and was rewarded with the feel of her sheathing him. To say he was jubilant would be an understatement. His fingers dug into her hips, urging Henrietta to move. She began to rock back and forth along his shaft from base to tip and back again. It was near torture to indulge her wish for control. Palms flattened against his chest, Henrietta raised herself into a sitting position, raking her fingertips over each rib. He wanted her to continue touching him but she rested her hands upon her thighs. She raised up on her knees and then sank back down, taking every inch of his cock inside her and intensifying the friction with small circular motions. Exerting what little control he had left, Walter refrained from bucking and pumping into her until he spilled his seed. She reached behind her, sliding one hand down to cup his balls. The added stimulation sent him over the edge. He dug his fingers into her hips and plunged into her. Each hard thrust extracted a pleasured moan from Henrietta. He continued until she collapsed on top of him, spent.

Lifting her forehead off his chest, Henrietta narrowed her gaze at him and then reached between them. Her fingers brushed against his slick, engorged manhood. "You are still...how are you...?" Her eyebrows rose in question.

He rolled his eyes towards the ceiling, praying she wouldn't press him for an answer. There was no explanation except for that now he was fully engulfed by her, his body was reluctant for the experience to end. His blood still pumped in eager anticipation.

Henrietta rocked her hips and grinned at him. "Again?"

"Aye, but this time, I shall do all the work." He rolled her onto her back and trailed kisses along her collar bone before mimicking her earlier moves, flicking his tongue over her nipple.

Walter slipped his hand between her legs and pressed the heel of his palm against her core. He needed to know if she was as close to finding her release again as he was. When she moaned and ground against him, he was prepared. He slid two fingers into her and tapped his thumb over her sensitive nub.

She tugged on his hair. "Walter. I want you."

It wasn't the three words he longed to hear her say. She hadn't said them in return when he had uttered them earlier, but it was a step closer. He settled himself between her legs and entered her. He slipped a hand under one of her knees and raised her leg until her thigh touched her chest, allowing him to deeper access. Fully seated in her, he rotated his hips.

She grabbed him by the shoulders. "Walter, stop torturing me."

Withholding his own release was torture for him too. She lifted her hips to meet his and he increased the tempo until she called out his name. For a second time, he couldn't stand the thought of leaving her and he spilled his seed deep inside the woman he loved.

Flopping next to Henrietta, Walter lay on his side, his arm supporting his sleepy head. "I'll need to rest before I leave, but I promise to depart before the first rays of light."

Henrietta nodded. "I trust you." She turned over and curled up against him, her back to his chest, legs intertwined. Her breathing evened out before sleep took him. He didn't want to have to leave. He didn't want to sneak about in the early morning hours. But the only way that would be possible was if Henrietta agreed to marry a second time.

CHAPTER TWENTY

*T*he next morning, Henrietta cradled baby Abigail Drummond close to her chest as she paced in front of an exhausted Theo. The curtains in the master chamber had been drawn shut to prevent daylight from seeping in. Henrietta completed another circuit of the room before coming to stand next to Theo. "You, my dear, need rest. I'll take this little one for a spell."

"Bring Abby back when she's hungry. I've dismissed the wet nurse Graham hired." Theo sank back against the wall of pillows at her back.

Henrietta rocked Abigail, who twisted towards her mama's voice. "Why did you do that?"

Eyes closed, Theo answered, "Abby latched on right away and I nursed her myself. She needs me and I need her. I won't let another do what I believe is my responsibility."

Theo yawned, her head rolling to the side to rest against the pillows. Henrietta stepped away from the bed. If she remained too close, Abigail might wail and demand to be fed again. Muttering more to herself than to Theo, Henrietta said, "You never have, my dear. I suppose I shouldn't be surprised."

Half asleep, Theo murmured, "Did *you* employ a wet nurse?"

Whirling around, Henrietta smiled at her niece who was snuggling down under the covers. "Good gracious, no." Henrietta placed a kiss on the baby's head. "I treasured those moments alone with Landon and then Christopher."

"I feel a strong need to protect and hold Abby." Theo smiled. "When she feeds, it creates a bond so strong, I've never felt with another before. Not even Graham."

"You shall be a wonderful mama." Henrietta stepped forward to place a quick kiss upon the top of Theo's head. "Rest. I promise to return with Abigail later."

Stealing the baby away to her rooms, Henrietta cooed at the infant until she fell fast asleep in her arms. Sinking into the winged back chair in front of the fire, she leaned back to admire her great-niece. "You may bear Archbroke's family name, Drummond, but you have Neale blood running through your veins. Neales are notorious for never following the rules, and I shall expect the same from you."

Still asleep, the baby smiled up at her. A warmth spread in her chest. Henrietta should be content with her lot. Ready to join George if that was to be her fate. Not dreaming of embarking upon another adventure with Walter. The memories of laying abed in the man's arms made her feel young again. She wasn't dead yet. But what was it she wanted—a private affair with the man she'd cared for as a girl and lusted after as a widow? Or would she be daring and claim the feeling she recognized as love? She may not have Neale blood in her veins, but she always felt more akin to them than her own family. Resting her head back, she closed her eyes and attempted to envision a future with Walter.

HENRIETTA BOLTED UPRIGHT, banishing the horrible images of women tittering behind fans, muttering, "Selfish... Stolen... Scandal."

Abigail remained blissfully asleep. But Henrietta's heart raced. Scooting to the edge of the chair, she rolled to her feet, but the jostling woke up Abigail with a start and the air filled with her protests.

"Shh." Henrietta bounced the baby as her feet hurried down the halls to the master chambers.

Theo was already out of bed with her robe on when Henrietta handed over the wailing child. Instantly the baby nuzzled against Theo, seeking out sustenance. Theo padded back to the bed where maids were fluffing pillows and straightening the linens.

Bent over her child, Theo said, "My, you have hearty lungs." She released the tie of her nightgown at the neck and settle the babe to her breast. "Thank you. After resting I don't feel half dead."

"It is why I agreed to reside here, under your husband's roof."

"Graham is not a beast..."

"He's an Archbroke. I'll grant you he has transformed somewhat; however, the true test will be how he will be with Abigail."

"I think you shall be in for a surprise, dear Aunt Henri."

"Humph."

"Shouldn't you be getting ready for this evening's affair?"

"I'm doubtful our scheme shall work."

"Archbroke will escort you to our box. His family will be there in full support, along with the Marquess of Harrington; his Grace, the Duke of Fairmont; and their lovely wives, Grace and Elise. Landon has confirmed Prinny shall be present tonight and hence Lady Irene's reentrance will be well timed."

"Walter has done a fine job of eliminating speculation as to Otterman's financial distress, and Lady Irene, according to my sources, has taken up residence at Otterman's townhouse without much fuss."

"How Otterman was so fortunate to find a woman as intelligent and strong willed as Lady Irene for a wife is still a conundrum to me. She possesses the characteristics to strengthen that family line; they may survive after all."

Abigail's half-closed lids popped back open as Theo repositioned her to suckle on the other breast.

"Perhaps we should share a small repast before I depart."

"That is a grand idea." Theo's maid took the sleeping babe from her niece's arms. "Wallace, will you please ask Cook to prepare a tray for Aunt Henri and me?"

"Yes, my lady." Wallace bobbed and left the room with the baby.

As soon as the door closed, Theo's intelligent eyes fell upon Henrietta. "What is troubling you?" Theo shifted and made room for Henrietta to sit next to her upon the bed.

"Where shall I start?" Henrietta leaned back against the headboard and stared down at her hands clenched in her lap. "I'm uncertain if I will succeed in orchestrating a suitable match for Bertha. None of the gentlemen she mentioned appear to have any interest in remarrying. I want her to experience love—or at the very least genuine affection."

"Not everyone is as fortunate as our family."

"I don't believe it is by pure happenstance that we find our mates."

"Perhaps we are overlooking someone obvious."

Theo was right. She needed to be on the lookout for a gentleman who may be admiring Bertha from the shadows. She should consult Walter.

Wallace entered with a tray and placed it on the table close to fireplace in Theo's bedchamber. "Cook and the staff are taking their fill of Lady Abigail. She has already charmed her way into their hearts."

Theo smiled like the proud mama she was. "I know she is in capable hands, I'm not worried."

Wallace curtsied and left them alone once more.

Henrietta rolled out of the bed and assisted Theo to don her robe. Together, they padded over to the table and settled into their chairs. Theo reached for the pot of tea but winced.

Henrietta swiftly shooed Theo to sit back. "You are still recovering. Let me." She poured them tea and continued, "Without you present tonight, it will be up to Bronwyn and me to manage both the scouting expedition for Bertha and ensuring Lady Irene's reentrance is a success."

"Might I suggest you allow Bronwyn to handle Lady Bertha's dilemma while you oversee Lady Irene."

"Do you think that wise?"

"You can't oversee both, and Bronwyn is a keen observer."

"Yes, you are correct." Henrietta munched on an egg and cress sandwich.

Theo, as always, was right. Archbroke and Landon would have their hands full dealing with Prinny this eve. The uncertainty surrounding the king's health, coupled with Prinny's increasing unpopularity due to his continued dastardly immoral behavior and poor treat-ment of his wife, had led to a number of threats resurfac-ing. Threats both Archbroke and Landon took most seriously.

Henrietta lifted her napkin to her mouth. "Hmm... that still leaves the matter of identifying someone suitable for Nicholas."

"The solution to that is simple; Lord Weathersbee—"

Mid-chew, Henrietta caught Theo staring at her collar bone.

"Aunt Henri, do I need to instruct the maids to check your bed linens for mites?"

A frisson of embarrassment rolled down Henrietta's spine. "No need." She adjusted her gown. She'd have to remember to wear a shawl this evening.

"Does Weathersbee make you happy?" Theo asked.

Happy. Youthful. Giddy. Walter made her feel all those things and more. The combination of emotions he conjured within her was far more complex than Henrietta was ready to examine. Henrietta's steadied her hand and lifted her teacup. "Yes." She took another sip and added, "I rather enjoy his company."

"Apparently so." Theo snorted. "But why do I sense you are not totally at peace?"

"Because you are entirely too perceptive." She had been widowed at fairly young age, granting her freedom to do as she pleased. Prior to Walter, no man had ever tempted her to consider the possibility of relinquishing her independence. "As a widow, there are a multitude of issues to be considered."

Brows furrowed Theo said, "Either I need more rest, or having given birth has muddled my mind. I don't understand your conundrum. It seems to me a wonderful position to be in. No societal pressures to marry. Everyone understands and accepts Weathersbee to be a confirmed bachelor."

"Walter mentioned he was no longer willing to love

me from a distance. What if he wishes for more than I am willing to give?"

With the assistance of Theo's papa, and the Network, Henrietta had employed unconventional methods such as establishing accounts under fictional male names merely to ensure she was able to participate in stock schemes and business ventures that most women were not privy to. She was no financial wizard like Landon, but it had been enough to ensure she never needed to seek out assistance from others. To place her ownership in the family law firm in jeopardy and relinquish control by legally binding herself to another was simply out of the question.

"Weathersbee is an extremely intelligent man. I believe he is wise enough to understand. Was it not you who advised me to simply speak from the heart?"

"Aye. I might have conveyed that message a time or two. However, following one's own advice is not as easy as issuing it."

Theo smiled behind her cup. Blast. Theo was right; she'd have to speak with Walter and tell him the truth—she was in love with him.

CHAPTER TWENTY-ONE

*T*he frisson of energy in the air was tangible. The Archbroke box was crammed with PORFs, every member on alert and prepared to deal with any potential threat to the Prince Regent who was milling about in the box, ogling the female theatre attendees below and chatting to Archbroke who stood close by.

A dark, foreboding feeling seeped into Henrietta's bones. She scanned the crowd for Walter and his nephew. There was no sign of either of them or Lord and Lady Otterman.

Bronwyn, who stood next to Henrietta, whispered from behind her fan. "They are late."

"The curtain never goes up on schedule, and the performance shall remain delayed until Prinny decides to cease milling about and take his seat." Henrietta squeezed her reticule. Walter considered being on time late, so for him to be delayed meant something beyond his control had prevented their party from arriving. Henrietta tried to calm her breathing. Her newfound feelings for the man were most bothersome and affecting her duties.

Bronwyn furiously waved her fan about. The fine wisps of hair that escaped her elegant coiffure fluttered, creating a halo effect. "Aye, and Archbroke is doing a marvelous job of distracting the Prince Regent." Raised as a Network member in servitude to PORFs, Bronwyn continued to idolize Archbroke and always spoke of him with deference.

Henrietta considered her nephew by marriage and replied, "He does have his strengths."

"You may not be fond of how much time he devotes to his responsibilities, but you cannot deny he loves Theo above all else."

"He should be at home with his wife and baby."

"That would upset Theo, and he hates it when his wife is unhappy." Bronwyn snapped her fan closed and let it dangle from her wrist. "I believe that to be a trait the men we love all share—the desire to see us happy." Bronwyn shifted slightly to the side, allowing Henrietta full view of Walter and the small party that was approaching the box.

"My, you have keen hearing," Henrietta remarked.

Bronwyn smiled and linked her arm through Henrietta's, and together they made their way to stand next to the new arrivals.

Henrietta greeted, "Lord Otterman. Lady Otterman, Lord Weathersbee and Lord Darlington."

Lady Otterman sank into a graceful curtsy. "Lady Henrietta. Countess Hadfield."

Formalities complete, Henrietta slid a glance at the man she had been anxiously awaiting. Walter winked at her, making her blush like she was nineteen once more. One by one, the gentlemen executed elegant bows in greeting. Ready for the evening events to commence, Henrietta said, "Lady Otterman, please come join us. We were on our way to take our seats... at the front of the box."

Gliding next to Bronwyn, Lady Irene was all poise and confidence. The curious, disapproving stares of the ton from the other boxes appeared to have no ill effect upon her. Maneuvering through their box, Henrietta caught the Prince Regent summoning them with a flick of his finger. She sent up a prayer for patience and whispered, "We have been summoned."

Lady Irene responded, "His Royal Highness's gaze makes my skin crawl."

"Naught to fear, you are married and surrounded by friends," Henrietta lied.

Sinking into a deep curtsy, Lady Irene took the Prince Regent's offered hand and rose.

The Prince Regent ignored the rest of them. "Archbroke, who is this delightful guest of yours?"

Dutifully, Archbroke stepped forward and said, "Your Highness, may I present to you Lord Otterman's wife, Lady Irene."

"Otterman is a fool to have left your side."

"I'm right here, Your Royal Highness." Lord

Otterman stepped forward, and Lady Irene shifted closer to Otterman in a public display of support for her husband.

Prinny's gaze narrowed before he slapped a hand upon Otterman's shoulder. "Come, you and your lovely wife must join me in the Royal box this eve."

The Prince Regent pivoted and made his way to his box. His contingent lined up in order of rank with Archbroke right behind Prinny.

Lady Irene grasped Henrietta's hand. "This is not the plan."

"No, it is certainly not. However, you will keep your chin up and stay close to Otterman." Henrietta squeezed Lady Irene's hand.

Waiting to join the end of the line, Lady Irene flipped her fan open and raised it to just below her chin. "My mama defied my papa and came for tea this afternoon."

Lady Irene's mama, Lady Vanessa, was not known for rebelling. Which confirmed Henrietta's belief that appearances could be quite deceiving, especially amongst the ton. Her own mama had been regarded as the perfect duchess. Yet at home, her mama and papa's relationship was anything but ideal. Even so, her mama had not once dared to contact Henrietta, even after the death of both George and Henrietta's papa. Her mama's actions and the continued refusal of her siblings to acknowledge her ate at Henrietta's soul. For reasons Henrietta had yet to understand, she had been deemed unworthy of their love. Henrietta silently vowed to do everything in her power to protect Lady Irene from the anguish she'd experienced.

Choking down the lump in her throat, Henrietta steeled her voice and asked, "How was the visit with your mama?"

Lady Irene's eyes pooled with moisture. "Mama made it quite clear she had not come to see me, but her grandchild."

Henrietta replied, "That must have been painful, my dear. You are doing remarkably well this eve and I, for one, am extremely proud of you."

Lady Irene dipped her head and raised her fan to hide behind. Expecting tears rolling down the woman's cheeks, Henrietta was shocked to see Lady Irene's eyes were clear and sparkled with determination. "It is you, Lady Henrietta, who gives me courage to get through this eve. You inspire me to go about with the self-knowledge that I am worthy of love and respect. Otterman does love me, and with time and patience and of course your kind support, I shall regain the respect of my peers... and if not... to hell with them."

Henrietta blushed. "I am honored to be your champion, Lady Irene. Now off you go." She nodded to Otterman, who had his arm at the ready to escort his wife. The couple were the last in the long procession. Lady Irene securing a coveted invitation to the Royal box was a feat. It would prompt more gossip, but if handled correctly it should work in their favor.

Her nose twitched at the familiar scent of parchment and ink mixed with sandalwood. She swiveled and found herself face-to-face with Walter, their lips inches from each other. It was insane to consider kissing Walter here and now, but her mind raced with images of them naked and in bed.

Walter leaned away from her and placed a socially acceptable amount of space between them. "I apologize for our late arrival."

"No need to apologize to me." She took his arm and together they made their way to the front row of seats of Archbroke's box.

"From whom should I be seeking forgiveness?"

"That would be Archbroke, who was left to entertain the Prince Regent until your arrival."

"Ah, poor Archbroke. Prinny has definitely raised the ire of many. Launching formal investigations into his wife's personal affairs. Declaring his intentions to seek a divorce, to ensure she never becomes queen. While he has been seen regularly visiting the woman he illegitimately married."

Henrietta snapped shut her mouth, which had fallen open at Walter's uncensored reply. She took her seat and waited for him to do the same. Frowning behind the program she'd opened, she asked, "Are you one of the many who are angered by the actions of our Prince Regent?"

"A man who denies his wife the right to see her own child does not have the markings of a great ruler."

"I wholeheartedly agree. Regardless of our personal opinions, I and other members of our family have sworn oaths to protect the man against all harm."

189

Walter glanced over to where Archbroke was slowly edging the Prince Regent to his seat, but Prinny was in no rush to have the evening's entertainment commence. "Do you ever imagine Archbroke fantasizing about strangling Prinny himself?"

Henrietta grinned. "Oh, I believe my dear nephew-in-law has imagined far worse."

A low growl came from behind Walter. Nicholas's gaze was trained on the box diagonally opposite. Lady Bertha, Miss Marina White, and two of their male family members were all guests of Lord Bartram. Perhaps the gentleman might be interested in remarrying. But when Henrietta raised her spying glasses, it wasn't Lord Bartram who was doting upon Bertha, it was his cousin Mr. Ainsworth. To Henrietta's dismay, both Lady Bertha and Miss White wore expressions of strain and sadness. Particularly Marina, who was trapped in between her two male relations. Both held an evil gleam in their eyes. Tendrils of dread and fear ran down Henrietta's spine. She had seen the same wicked glimmer in the men's gazes years before, when they were boys tormenting a poor caged rabbit. She had saved that poor injured creature, and she was going to save Bertha and Marina this eve.

Henrietta shifted and turned around to whisper. "Lord Darlington, what are you doing still sitting there? Go find Landon and escort them over here."

Nicholas blinked as her orders sank in. "Yes, my lady." He rose to do her bidding.

Walter rose and urged Henrietta to do the same. "I

believe an invitation from you, my dear, would be more appropriate. Allow me to escort you."

Henrietta frowned. Walter's logic was sound, as she was related to Archbroke, but Bertha's brother Bartholomew was the malicious sort. He would simply ignore Henrietta and give her the cut direct, as a sign of fidelity to the ducal family that continued to reject her.

Walter leaned in. "Trust me." He glanced at Nicholas and then to Lady Irene. Nicholas nodded in acknowledgment of Walter's unspoken orders to remain in the box.

Henrietta took Walter's arm. "You had best be right about this. We are jeopardizing more than one woman's future."

No sooner had the curtain flapped closed behind them than a hand upon her shoulder halted her movements. "Mama. Where are you going?" Hmph. Of all moments, Landon decided to prove himself capable of moving about undetected.

She spun to face her son. "To rescue Bertha and Miss White."

"Could you endeavor to limit the number of tasks we undertake this eve?" He dropped his hand and waved for her to proceed him.

"Landon Neale. Bertha is a close friend; I won't let her suffer."

"Of course, Mama, but we shan't always be able to come to everyone's aid." When had her son grown into such a wise man? She gave him a wink and allowed Walter to escort her to Lord Bartram's box.

CHAPTER TWENTY-TWO

*H*aving Henrietta walking next to him, with her hand upon his arm, was an experience Walter had dreamt of often but never believed possible. His steps, lighter than ever before, carried them through the theatre with speed. The determined set of her lips had Walter grinning. He admired Henrietta's loyalty and fierceness.

Landon hastened to overtake them just before they reached Lord Bertram's box. A footman held the curtain back for them.

As they entered, Henrietta was slightly hidden behind Landon. Lady Bertha spotted Walter and greeted him with a pretty smile that quickly disappeared at the sight of Henrietta. A peculiar response given they were there to save her.

"Lord Hadfield. Lord Weathersbee. Henrietta. How lovely to see you all this eve." Lady Bertha looked about and Miss White came to stand next to her cousin.

Henrietta replied, "We have been asked to extend an invitation to you and Miss White to join us in Lord Archbroke's box."

Miss White's eyes went wide and her stiff shoulders relaxed before her gaze collided with Lady Bertha's conflicted features.

Lady Bertha's internal debate was clear for all to see. She had always been one you could read easily, and it was for that reason Walter had tempered his interactions with the woman for years. He wasn't blind. He'd known of her interest in him, but he wasn't one to cause hurt to another. Unrequited love was excruciatingly painful.

Henrietta leaned in closer. "What is the matter, Bertha? I've come to rescue you and Miss White."

Lady Bertha nodded. She turned to address her brother, who was scowling at their party. "Brother, Marina and I shall enjoy this evening's performance from Lord Archbroke's box." Lady Bertha didn't wait for a response, but grabbed Miss White's hand and marched out.

Henrietta was close on her friend's heels, her whispered plea barely reaching his ears. "Bertha."

Lady Bertha rounded upon Henrietta, and only Henrietta's quick reaction prevented them from colliding. "You! You are not my friend."

Walter remained close but far enough away to afford the ladies some privacy.

Henrietta's brows shot up. Her spine stiffened and she asked, "What are you saying?"

"While I am grateful you rescued us from

Bartholomew and the awful Lord Bertram, I detest being lied to." Lady Bertha's ire disappeared for a moment before returning. "Did you know Lord Bertram hasn't seen his children since last March? He's not wallowing in grief. He's been lying about with his mistress. To think I thought he might be someone I could come to care for." All Lady Bertha's energy seemed to seep from her. Bent head, rounded shoulders, she continued, "That horrid man informed me he'd not give up his mistress but would quite happily see to ensuring our wedding was valid prior to shipping me off to his country estate." Hands covering her face, she spoke the last few words in sobs.

Walter shifted his weight to his back foot and Landon glanced at him with a shrug. Henrietta wrapped her arms about Lady Bertha.

Except Lady Bertha pulled away and glared. "Don't. You are not to comfort me. You've already had a husband." Lady Bertha pointed to a stunned Landon. "Raised two strapping boys. You could have simply told me you wanted Weathersbee for yourself."

Lady Bertha grabbed Miss White and marched away, leaving a stunned and ghostly white Henrietta behind.

Walter turned to Landon. "Take your mother home. I'll take care of matters."

Lengthening his stride to catch up to the women, Walter was near parallel when Nicholas darted out from the box and ran headlong into Miss White. His nephew caught the girl stumbling backwards and righted her with speed and care.

"Are you all right, Miss White?"

Cheeks a bright red, Marina nodded.

"Please allow me to escort you inside." Nicholas placed her shaking hand upon his arm and the pair disappeared into the box.

Walter turned and said, "Lady Bertha, a moment of your time, please."

Moisture filled the woman's eyes. His chest ached at the sight of the woman's upset. He shifted to block her from the view of others and retrieved a handkerchief, which he handed to Lady Bertha.

She took the clean white linen. "My thanks."

He hated the fact that it was his rejection that caused Lady Bertha's pain. "I've loved Henrietta since I was a lad. Believe me, I fully understand how you feel. I've wanted, tried to love others, but my heart refuses to listen to reason."

"Henrietta is rather loveable." Lady Bertha gave him a weak smile. "I didn't really mean all those things…" He narrowed his gaze and Lady Bertha added, "Well, maybe a little. I was angry, but nonetheless I shouldn't have…"

"I'm certain Henrietta will understand once you explain." He winged his arm. "I'm sorry I cannot return your regard, but perhaps we can still enjoy the evening's performance as friends."

"Yes, I'd like for us to be friends. Once Hen forgives me, I expect we shall be spending more time in each other's presence."

THE PERFORMANCE WAS BRILLIANT. The talented Sienna Betonni even had Prinny enraptured for a period. However, Walter's mind was rehearsing what he was to say to Henrietta when he next spoke to her—alone. Miss White's sharp inhale brought his attention back to the pair seated in front of him. A palpable tension rolled off his nephew's shoulders and Walter narrowed his gaze upon Nicholas. The young couple were like magnets. Face-to-face they were tangibly drawn to one another, but with Miss White's head turned in the opposite direction, it was as if Nicholas was being prevented from getting closer by an invisible force. Walter empathized with his nephew's plight—to have a woman within reach yet not close enough.

Lady Bertha broke his concentration, inquiring, "Lord Weathersbee, what do you know of Mr. Ainsworth?"

"He's a fine botanist and is reported to be an excellent marksman. Why do you ask?"

"No particular reason."

"He's not in line to inherit a title."

"Neither was George when Henrietta married him, and they..." She clapped her hand over her mouth and then said, "I'm sorry, Lord Weathersbee; that was extremely insensitive of me."

"No need to apologize. George loved Henrietta. I was happy for them both."

"You are remarkably understanding."

"I think not. I kept my friendship with George a secret for years and avoided gatherings if there was even the remotest possibility of seeing them together. It was extremely difficult and painful."

"To keep secrets."

He shook his head. "To love someone knowing there was no possibility of them returning the sentiment."

"But Hen does love you. I saw it this evening from Lord Bertram's box."

"Even so, she is four years my senior; to love openly will only cause gossip and scandal."

"Pfft. Hen is a widow. She can do as she pleases, and if her family has no objections, the only obstacle I foresee is yourself."

CHAPTER TWENTY-THREE

*P*acing the length of her bed chambers, Henrietta counted three extra steps. Apparently while the layout was the same as her rooms at the Hadfield townhouse, Archbroke's was slightly larger. The PORF families were supposed to be equals, yet the more she learned of the secret society she married into, the more apparent it was that reality did not mirror the original designs of its creators. Greed—man's folly and the reason for most failed schemes. Bertha's insults implied that *she* was acting with greed, wanting to experience love a second time. Except loving Walter was an entirely different experience at the age of one-and-fifty.

Henrietta's heels struck a hollow board on the floor. She paused and stared at the rug beneath her. Bending to get down on her hands and knees, Henrietta rolled the worn material back. Her hands shook slightly as she rocked the wooden plank to dislodge the dust sealing it in place. Discovering and gathering information had been a key element to Henrietta's recovery from George's death. The board gave way to reveal an empty hidden compartment. She stuck her hand in to feel about the cavity. Experience had taught her that relying on sight alone could be a very dangerous mistake. Her heart stopped at the sound of the door of the secret passage opening. Jumping to her feet, Henrietta hid the flooring behind her. She slowly turned around to face her visitor. She exhaled. The figure in the entrance was neither Walter nor Theo. It was Archbroke.

Her nephew-in-law stepped forward and came to stand before her. "I was worried about you when you failed to return to the box this eve." He held out his hand.

Without a word, she handed over the piece of wood that was evidence of her snooping. "I had Landon's escort. No need to have been concerned."

He hunkered down and replaced the board before repositioning the rug to its original position. "My grandmama was fond of stashing her love letters here." He glanced down briefly before meeting her gaze once more. "She was extremely discreet. In her later years, she dallied with many a gentleman who was... well... *significantly* younger than herself. She died a fortunate woman."

Archbroke offering her advice on love was a bizarre experience. Blast the man. He was correct—discretion was key if she dared to continue her relationship with Walter.

Archbroke tugged at his meticulously tied cravat fashioned of gamboge silk. "It's been brought to my attention that I've failed to convey my sentiments toward you. Specifically, my gratitude for your willingness to reside here in my home. Theo needs you." He stood and held out his hand. "We need you."

She placed her hand in his and slowly rose. "Bah. You don't need anyone." Henrietta worried for her niece. Theo had a lifetime of challenges in store for her with Archbroke as husband. The man resisted change and held onto traditional theorems that were antiquated. He was the exact opposite of a Hadfield.

"For once, my dear aunt, you are mistaken." He shook his head and smiled. A genuine curve of the lips Henrietta had only ever seen emerge in the presence of Theo.

Henrietta asked, "Pray tell, how is it *you* need *me*?"

"Without your constant assessing eyes, I might fall into terrible old habits." He sighed, and his shoulders sagged as if the burden of what he was about to share was heavier than he cared to admit. "I was raised to believe my oath as a PORF and my role as Home Secretary were everything. Anything else was a distraction. When in fact family is what is most important. Without Theo, I never would have experienced love; but without you, I would lose it all." Hands clasped behind his back, Archbroke's cool blue stare bored into her.

She shouldn't be shocked by his insightful confession —the man was a bloody genius. Henrietta's dazed mind raced. She took in Archbroke's open and honest features. For this brief moment, it appeared he was willing to lower the shield he had devised to protect himself and the secrets inherent to being a PORF.

To reward his candidness, Henrietta shared, "When I married into the Hadfield family, I believed the qualities that made me unique were of value. All these years I've attempted to prove myself worthy of the mark."

Archbroke rolled back his shoulders, adopting his normal authoritative no-nonsense pose. "And you certainly have. Henrietta, you raised Landon, a man I'm honored to call Head PORF. It is a role that carries a heavy burden, yet he does so with humility and honor. That is all due to you." There was no cynicism in his tone, only pure sincerity. "Your boys and Theo are grown and happily married. I hope my children will have the benefit of your guidance for years to come, but it is time for you to lead a life with yourself as your sole purpose. Enjoy every day you are given."

Bertha's accusations railed to the forefront of her mind. Henrietta replied, "I've already led a full life."

"You're not dead yet." Archbroke gave her one of his most serious stares. "You are a Hadfield—don't fail the legacy now. Hadfields are proponents of love, are they not?"

"George always said 'to love is to live.'"

With a nod, Archbroke declared, "Then it is settled."

"What is?" Conversing with a mastermind that expected everyone around him to keep up was exhausting.

Archbroke shrugged. "You are assigned to overseeing the matter of Lord Weathersbee."

Blaming it on her lack of sleep, she blinked at her austere-looking nephew-in-law. "I beg your pardon."

"You shall ensure Weathersbee's continued silence regarding our existence. In doing so, I expect you to allow him the honor of loving you as you love him." He returned to the entrance of the secret passageway. "Unless you choose to decline the assignment, and then I shall have to see to it he…"

"Heavens, no! I accept."

"Grand. Best keep the man close." With a wink, Archbroke disappeared into the dark passage.

She'd never failed to fulfill her duties as a PORF and guard the family secrets, and she wasn't about to fail now.

Instead of the door sliding to a close, it flung open. With a clever retort to Archbroke's parting comment on the tip of her tongue, Henrietta gasped when Walter instead of Archbroke appeared. "How did you get past Archbroke without detection? Never mind that; why are you here?"

Ignoring her question, Walter sealed the door closed and strode to the window to peek out from behind the curtains. She tapped her toe softly as she counted to ten.

On the count of twelve, Walter left his post by the window and came to stand inches away from her. His actions told her he'd been trained by someone as to how to go about undetected. George! Walter's actions mirrored her own, the same precautions her deceased husband had insisted she master. Slowly, she tilted her head up to meet his gaze. A flash of admission in his warm brown eyes.

Walter opened his mouth and then shut it. He

repeated the action twice before he said, "I've come to set matters straight."

She really needed to get some sleep. Twice in the span of an hour, she found herself unable to follow another's thoughts.

Walter took her hand and guided her over to the settee in front of the dying fire. His grip was light, not his usual warm clasp that engulfed her hand and made her feel safe. She fiddled with the creases of material that gathered at her waist while he stoked the flames. Walter rubbed his back as if it was aching. Henrietta was not alone in feeling the effects of their age. She halted her anxious movements and pressed her hand flat against her stomach to settle the fluttering inside that had begun as soon as Walter had entered her chamber.

When he turned to face her, she was about to inquire as to what ailed him, but the sadness in his eyes had her holding her tongue. Her hands began to sweat as her mind played out several scenarios of how Walter spent the evening with Bertha. The fluttering in her stomach was now a dull ache. He sat alongside Henrietta and his knee brushed up against hers. Henrietta held her breath in anticipation of the learning what caused Walter such torment. After all, he had said he was here to set matters between them straight. Gathering every ounce of patience, she clasped her hands tightly in her lap.

Walter reached over and rested one of his large hands over hers. His thumb stroked the back of her hand. "For years, I've suspected Lady Bertha may have held an affection for me..."

She didn't want to hear the rest. Henrietta took his hand in hers and said, "There is no need to explain anything to me."

Before she could utter another word, he kissed her. His tongue sought entrance and she granted it. The flicker of his tongue reminded her of the exquisite night of pleasure he had given her. She wanted to return the favor and give him the same sexual gratification. She slid her lips over his jaw and up to nip at his ear.

Walter pulled her lips back to his, and then when she was left breathless and wanting, he leaned back and said, "We are going to have a long discussion, you and I. I need you to agree to hold your tongue. At least long enough for me to explain everything."

A little dazed from his kisses, she simply nodded. He kissed her like a passionate lover, not someone who was about to crush her hopes of experiencing the love of a man a second time.

"I have loved you every day since you entered my life." Walter ran his hands down her arms and held her hands in his. "When we came to London the year of your coming out, I had an extravagant plan for you to remain unwed until I came of age. But then George hunted me down the same day he laid eyes upon you." Face-to-face with her, he paused and searched her features, for what she wasn't sure.

He inhaled deeply. "George kindly exploited the faults of my scheme and painted for me a different life for you. A life he could provide for you that I couldn't. Your husband was extremely persuasive, but it wasn't his arguments that made me trust him, it was the way he wore his emotions upon his sleeve and left me with no doubt that he'd love and cherish you." Walter smiled.

It wasn't a smile for her benefit. Walter clearly had admired and cared for George.

Walter patted her hand. "George quizzed me for hours upon hours during our first meeting on all sort of various topics, but none specifically about you. At the time I hadn't realized his true intent. It was only years later, after knowing him, that I understood his purpose. He was studying me. My reactions to the questions combined with my responses told him exactly how best to approach and converse with you."

George always conducted his affairs with multiple purposes, but why question Walter? Brows creased, she admitted, "I don't understand."

Walter chuckled. "I see I'm not explaining very well. George was a PORF, a descendent from the Hadfield line trained to obtain valuable information about others without being noticed. Unconsciously, each of my responses always alluded to your preferences." He smiled. "Let me provide you an example. He had inquired as to my thoughts upon returning to Eton for another semester. Inevitably, my answer incorporated your feelings upon the inequity of education for girls versus boys, and the fact I hated to be away from you."

"That's not what I meant. I comprehend how he gained insight into me, but George was a master at multitasking. For what other purpose were his inquiries made?

205

You were fourteen at the time." She turned her hand over to interlace their fingers.

He squeezed her hand once more. "Ahh... George was assessing me and my skills."

"Your skills?"

"Aye. My ability to retain and recall detailed conversations." He shifted and hauled her to sit across his lap before he continued, "George was wise to the fact that as a third son, no one took note if I was or wasn't present. Your husband pointed out that men in general tended to underestimate women and minors. And like you, I longed for adventure and challenges. My friendship with George was a miracle. Without his aid, I'd not have survived Eton nor Cambridge. Without the added challenge of George's schemes, my education would have merely consisted of words upon a page. I'd not have learned the nuances of speech, interpreting others' facial expressions, and much more."

Henrietta leaned against his shoulder and sighed. "George gave you what he gave me—a purpose to live."

He hugged her close. "He was more a brother to me than those that shared my blood."

"Why did you keep it a secret from me?"

"Because I shared the same pain Bertha experienced tonight. An ache so deep in one's chest that you lash out at those that care for you. I loved you both, but I couldn't be in the same room as the two of you." He tilted his head to capture her gaze.

She shuddered. "Bertha hates me."

He shook his head. "She doesn't. She's stronger than

me. Even said she hoped to be my friend since we would be in each other company once you forgave her."

Her back stiffened and she said, "Me, forgive *her*? It is I who should seek forgiveness."

"I don't believe we will have to worry much about Lady Bertha." His nimble fingers began working on the row of concealed clasps that had been sewn into the material to hold the seam of her gown together. No surprise he had become rather proficient at divesting her of her gowns.

Easing one arm out of her sleeve, she asked, "Why is that?"

"Mr. Ainsworth couldn't keep his eyes off her all evening." He placed a kiss upon her bare shoulder and assisted her to extricate her other arm from her dreaded gown.

Distracted by the warmth of Walter's breath against her neck, Henrietta struggled to recall the man's association. "Lord Bertram's cousin?"

"Aye." Walter eased the material over her hips and let the gown fall to the floor. "He is a good man. Nothing like his wastrel of an older brother."

Henrietta fingers played with the buttons on Walter's waistcoat. If Walter wasn't concerned, then Bertha was in good hands with Mr. Ainsworth. "What of Miss White?"

"Don't worry. I'll see to it Nicholas comes up to snuff."

She slipped a hand under his waistcoat and circled

his nipple with her forefinger. He placed a hand over hers, stilling her movements.

Walter said, "I overheard Archbroke's orders."

"Oh."

He kissed her brow. "Yes, I'm quite pleased you are to be my keeper..." He brought her hand up to rest at the side of his neck and placed his hands solidly on her waist to lift her so she could straddle him. Grinning, Walter added, "I'd feared Landon would undertake the task himself."

She angled her head to one side. "You are not annoyed?"

"Why would I be? I love you and wish to spend as much time with you as possible. Archbroke is no fool. He created a reason for others to believe. We know the truth and the actual cause for us to be together, and that is all that matters."

She leaned forward, her lips inches from his. "I love you, too."

CHAPTER TWENTY-FOUR

*R*eturning to Archbroke's townhouse with his nephew in tow at a respectable hour, Walter grinned as the knocker fell upon the front door. For three days, he'd spent his days at the office and his nights sneaking into the household through the back entrance.

Nicholas stood behind him. "Do you intend this be a short or a long visit?"

"That all depends upon you. Henrietta is curious as to how your search for a wife is faring."

The front door swung open, and they were greeted with the ruckus of children's laughter and Archbroke's roar mimicking some wild animal. Walter entered and gave the butler his coat, hat, and gloves. He waited for Nicholas to do the same, but his nephew still had not entered.

"Perhaps I should return later."

Walter grabbed the lad by the arm and pulled him into the foyer. "You can't delay the inevitable." He searched Nicholas's features, who was acting peculiar. "Henrietta isn't a dragon. She is quite harmless."

"It's not that, Uncle. It's..."

Henrietta appeared at the foot of the stairs. "Lord Darlington, how lovely to see you." She approached and gave Walter a kiss upon the cheek. "I'm glad you decided to take the morning off instead of hiding in the office today."

Nicholas bowed. "A good morn to you, Lady Henrietta."

Henrietta left Walter's side, linked her arm about Nicholas's, and steered him to the far drawing room, past the room where Archbroke was entertaining his nephew and niece who were in residence. Max and Claire were a delightful and extremely intelligent pair that both Theo and Graham doted upon as if they were their own. And the children adored their new cousin, always asking to hold the babe. Managing the Home Office, Archbroke was a stickler for order and tradition, but at home, he was an entirely different man. Walter enjoyed his visits to Archbroke's townhouse, both during the day and evenings. It was filled with warmth and laughter. No stodgy meals in the morn nor at supper, and Walter cherished the invitation to join them.

Sliding onto the settee next to Henrietta, Walter watched as Nicholas perched on the edge of the chair next to them. "Lad, pray tell what has you behaving like a man about to be hung?"

"It's Miss Marina White."

"Ah, the girl has caught your attention."

"No." He jumped to his feet and rounded the chair, grabbing the back with clenched hands. "How do I explain?"

Walter said, "Simply state the facts."

"The other night at the opera, Miss White was behaving shy and demure. Unlike our previous meetings where she boldly glared and declared her opinions. She wouldn't meet my gaze, and when Lady Bertha reached for her arm to leave, Marina flinched as if in pain.

"You fear for her well-being?"

Nicholas threw his hands in the air. "It's senseless. I'm fully aware she is quite capable of handling herself and others. Yet I have this gnawing feeling in the bottom of my stomach."

The door to the drawing room opened. Before the butler could announce their visitor, Miss White herself rushed into the room and stood before Henrietta.

Wringing her hands, Miss White said, "Aunt Henri, you must help." Since when had Miss White taken to calling Henrietta aunt?

Henrietta rose and embraced the girl, running a calming hand up and down her back as she sobbed into Henrietta's shoulder. "Hush. All will be well, but first you must tell me what has occurred."

"Aunt Bertha..." Marina pulled back and took a calming breath. "Aunt Bertha has run off with Mr. Ainsworth." Pulling a crumpled piece of parchment from her pocket, she handed it over to Henrietta. "She left me this note."

Nicholas left his post by the chair and came to stand next to Marina.

"Oh, Lord Darlington, I did not realize you were here." Just as his nephew had mentioned earlier, the girl cowered away from him. Nicholas would never harm a woman. Walter found the action rather insulting. He was about to join the trio when Henrietta glanced back and gave her head a little shake. In fact, she herself moved further away from the younger couple to stand by the far window. Eyes narrowed, she raised the parchment to the light and focused on reading its content.

His nephew shifted yet another inch closer to Miss White and a dark scowl settled upon his features. "Why is there face paint covering your pretty features?" He tipped up the girl's tear-streaked face. Even from the settee Walter could see the dark, yellowish tinge across the girl's cheekbone.

Nicholas pulled her to him. "Which of your blasted male relatives dared to touch you?"

The girl rocked her head side to side.

"I won't let them near you again," Nicholas declared.

Henrietta returned waving the letter about. "Bertha states you are to join her and Mr. Ainsworth. We merely need to..."

"She's not going anywhere." His nephew glared at Henrietta.

Walter jumped to his feet. "It's not up to you, Nicholas."

Miss White pulled back and stepped out of Nicholas's reach. She rolled her shoulders back and faced

Henrietta. "I came here today, in hopes, Aunt Henri, that you might recommend me for a position in Lord Archbroke's household—mayhap as a nursemaid."

The material of Nicholas's jacket was pulled taut across his back. All traces of the boy's patience evaporated. "Oh, no you're not. You shall not be in anyone's employ."

At Nicholas's arrogance, the self-assured young woman Walter had first met reemerged. Chin held high, hands firmly planted upon her hips, the girl said, "You have no say in the matter, Lord Darlington. Shouldn't you be taking *Lady* Emilie for a carriage ride?"

Walter and Henrietta glanced at each other and took a half step back. Miss White was small in stature, but she had a mean right hook and pointy elbows. It wouldn't do to be in the way if she decided to give Nicholas the solid wallop he deserved. The heavy emphasis on the honorifics was not lost on anyone. Especially not Nicholas, whose eyes had narrowed and lips had thinned into a severe line.

Miss White held her ground as his nephew took a step closer. "What gave you the impression I would be taking Lady Emilie anywhere?"

Walter had been absent from the Darlington residence for days, but surely if Nicholas was courting someone, his nephew would have informed him.

Bowing her head, Miss White answered, "Chatter among household staff is not uncommon, my lord." The reply was part mumble, part sigh.

Tilting Marina's chin up again, Nicholas said, "Then

213

you shan't miss the ill-informed household from which you heard these terrible lies."

Miss White blinked.

Walter smiled. If he was a wagering man, he'd bet his nephew was going to propose.

Instead of dropping to one knee or reaching for the woman, Nicholas barked, "Nor will you reside here as Archbroke's nanny. We shall marry."

Mouth agape, not a word came out of Miss White's mouth.

Slow to react to the hash of a proposal, Walter stood back while Henrietta wedged her way between the couple. "Lord Darlington. In Lady Bertha's absence, I claim full responsibility for Miss White's care. She is under my protection. And I can assure you, she will in no way be forced into marriage."

Nicholas bent and whispered in Henrietta's ear. What secrets was his nephew keeping from him these days?

Henrietta's spine stiffened. She pulled Marina aside to the other side of the room, clear out of earshot.

Walter asked, "What is going on? Are you in love with Miss White?"

"If what I feel for Miss White is love, then the poets have it all wrong. However, I do feel a need to protect the woman and I'm confident she'll provide me with a strong-willed, intelligent heir."

He stared at his nephew. "I apologize for raising you to hold such beliefs."

"Uncle. I've seen the pain of unrequited love. I will

not subject myself to such agony. Miss White doesn't love me, nor do I love her. It is a fine arrangement."

Walter wanted to state that the pain of failure he was currently experiencing was far worse than years of loving another from afar. But he knew it would fall upon deaf ears. Nicholas's jaw was set in determination. There was no changing the lad's mind.

Henrietta and Miss White rejoined them. Henrietta stepped forward. "It will take you at least three days or more to arrange matters. Miss White does not wish to return to her uncle's household, and..."

Nicholas reached into his breast pocket and withdrew a folded parchment. "Your family is not the only one who has access to the archbishop. I believe Miss White has the choice of either marrying me later this eve in a private ceremony held at a location of her choice, or we can set off for the border."

Henrietta snatched the paper from Nicholas's grasp. She unfolded it so he could view its contents along with her. His nephew's claims he did not love the girl were false. Nicholas's actions were that of a man fully in the depths of the emotion, even if he wasn't ready to admit to it.

"Miss White, it appears Lord Darlington is able to offer you an alternative to your own and Bertha's plans."

"May I see the special license?"

Henrietta handed over the sheet of parchment. Miss White's eyes swiftly ran over the document. "'Tis dated with yesterday's date."

"I apologize for my tardiness. However, your uncle

misinformed me. He insinuated that you and your cousin had left town to attend a house party in the country. He would not provide me with the details. I had hoped Lady Henrietta would be able to provide me the information I needed to locate you."

"You were looking for me?"

"Yes."

Marina refolded the parchment and handed it back to Nicholas. "I'll agree to wed you upon the condition you will honor your promise never to let my uncle near me again."

"Done. Are we to wed here or in Scotland, my dear?"

"I'd like to confer with Aunt Henri for a moment."

The two ladies once again huddled in the far corner.

"What did you say to Henrietta earlier?"

"I simply told her that I'd promise to protect and cherish Marina to the best of my abilities."

"The girl deserves to be loved."

"She has agreed to marry me, uncle. You should be happy. I'm fulfilling my duty. I'm to be wed as you wished, and you are fond of Marina, are you not?"

"I am."

"Then let's hope she opts for a quick ceremony in town. I'd prefer if you were in attendance at this momentous event of my life."

Henrietta rejoined them. "We'll hold the ceremony later this afternoon. I shall speak to Landon and Archbroke and will notify you of the location and exact time you are expected, Lord Darlington. I suggest you take yourself home and begin your own preparations." She turned to Walter. "You had best accompany him, make sure the household will be ready to receive its new mistress."

Henrietta tugged on his arm. He bent so she could whisper in his ear. "Might I suggest you bring a valise with you this eve. From experience, my advice is to never cohabitate with a newlywed couple.

"I shall take your words of wisdom to heart and be prepared." He nodded to Nicholas, and they took their leave. He was troubled by his nephew's view on marriage, but was at a loss as to how to help. Nicholas was a smart lad; he'd figure it out in time. The prospect of spending even an extra hour with Henrietta each night put a spring into his step as they left Archbroke's townhouse.

EPILOGUE

*S*ix weeks later...

Hands on her hips, Henrietta stared down at her traveling trunks. Theo was fully recovered from childbirth. It was time for her to retire to the country, to the dowager wing at Hadfield Hall. She was tasked to keep Bronwyn company, and out of trouble, until Landon could join her at the family estate. Henrietta tapped her toe against the wooden side of the box that contained the volumes that would have to keep her entertained and then froze. Leaving town and Walter was not ideal, but she hadn't managed to devise an alternative plan. Rooted to the spot, she waited for Walter to wrap his arms about her waist. Instead, lips grazed the back of her neck. She turned and leaned into the man who reminded her every day she was needed and loved. She might have outlived some of her peers, but she wasn't dead yet. In fact, Walter made her eager to experience each new day.

Walter lifted her chin and lowered his lips to hers.

His heart raced beneath her palm that was pressed flat against his chest.

Breathless, Henrietta rested her cheek over the back of her hand. "I shall miss you."

"We need to talk. I shan't be too far away."

Hope and confusion had her taking a step back. "I wasn't aware you had a country residence."

"I don't." Walter took her by the hand and led her to the small sitting area near the windows. "I took the liberty of seeking out a private meeting with your son and Archbroke."

"For what purpose?" She tugged her hand out of his grasp.

"I merely reminded them of your assigned task to ensure I keep certain details a secret." Walter remained smiling, almost smug.

She planted her hands back on her hips. "Walter Weathersbee, interfering in PORF business is not in your purview." Her brows shot up as she said, "Please tell me you did not seek out their permission for me to marry."

"Of course not." Walter's smile disappeared. A vertical crease between his eyebrows appeared. "I thought we were in agreement on the subject of marriage."

She hadn't meant to offend him. He was correct; a little over a week ago, they had openly agreed that a certificate of marriage would only complicate matters at their age, and there was no need as long as they both remained true to each other. She reached out to recapture his hand. "I apologize. We are."

Walter's shoulders relaxed a tad, but there remained a wariness in his gaze. "Landon has made arrangements for you to reside here in town, in your own residence."

"Why was I not consulted on the matter?"

Her brash reply banished all traces of uncertainty from Walter's features. The man even had the audacity to calmly sit and pat the seat cushion next to him. "Would you have preferred to spend the summer at Hadfield Hall instead of in town?" He leaned back and rested his arm along the back of the settee.

"You know my preferences. I wish to be with you." She flopped down upon the settee next to him and crossed her arms against her chest. "Did you say my *own* residence?" Turning to face Walter, she began to comprehend the limitless number opportunities of being alone with the man. Being mistress of her own residence would be a huge boon.

"Aye. Archbroke and Landon agreed with me that it would be perfectly reasonable for you to stay in Christopher's vacated townhouse during his absence. Its close proximity to the office means you will be able to keep an eye on me and my... activities." His fingers brushed against her shoulder.

She wanted to remain irritated at him, but Henrietta recognized the brilliance of his scheme.

Walter's fingers kneaded her tight shoulder muscles. "You know, my dear, I couldn't fathom being apart from you. I would follow you anywhere; however, Christopher left the responsibility of overseeing Neale & Sons to me. Until his return..."

She tilted her head to the side to rest on his shoulder. "I fully understand the situation."

"Are you not pleased with your new living arrangements?"

Releasing a half sigh and half moan, Henrietta shifted so that they were face-to-face. "When will men ever learn, women do not care to be managed?"

Lips curved into a smile, Walter replied, "Perhaps the day when the age of a woman compared to that of a man's no longer matters."

"Bah! Neither of us will live long enough to see such occurrences." She twisted and fell back to rest against his solid chest.

He wrapped his arm around her. "I apologize for not consulting you first."

"I realize you acted out of care and not selfishness."

His chest rumbled as he chuckled. "Ah, but I did act out of selfish need. I couldn't bear the thought of being apart from you. After all these years of waiting, I wasn't going to let us be separated. We may not be bound by marriage, but we are by love."

ALSO BY RACHEL ANN SMITH -
HISTORICAL

THE HADFIELDS

Book 1: Revealing a Rogue

For years she worked for him...

...and was loyal to a fault.

Why did she let herself yearn for a man, with whom she had
no future?

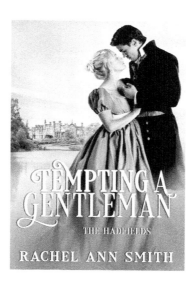

Book 2: Tempting a Gentleman

She runs a successful dress shop.

He's a talented barrister.

Will his skills as a lover or as a lawyer prevail?

AGENTS OF THE HOME OFFICE

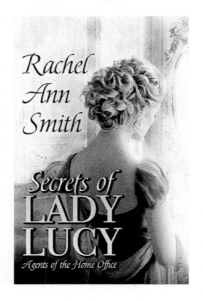

Book 1: Secrets of Lady Lucy

She is determined to foil an attempted kidnapping.

He is set on discovering her secrets.

When the ransom demand comes due—will it be for Lady
Lucy's heart?

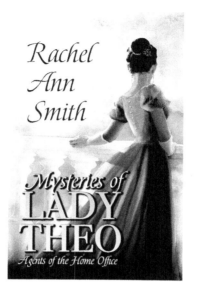

Book 2: Mysteries of Lady Theo

She inherited her family's duty to the Crown.

His duty to the Crown took priority.

Will the same duty that forced them together be what
ultimately drives them apart?

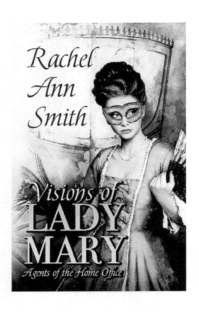

Book 3: Visions of Lady Mary

She wants a life of adventure.

He once called her a witch.

Will fate prevail or will Mary's stubbornness win out?

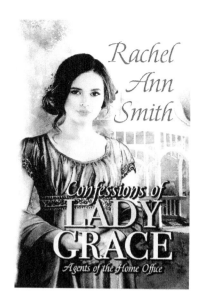

Book 4: Confessions of Lady Grace

She sacrificed her future to save his life.

He survived only to return home and find she is
betrothed to another.

Will her confessions set them both free?

Damien

I'm done with work and women.

Except there is a bikini clad blonde standing her ground
on *my* terrace.

Irene

What do you do after jilting a cheating fiancé at the altar?

Not fall in love with a man you nick name Mr. Merman.

Find out what happens when a reservation mix-up has these
two stuck together on a remote island.

ABOUT THE AUTHOR

RACHEL ANN SMITH writes steamy historical romances with a twist. Her debut series, Agents of the Home Office, features female protagonists that defy convention.

When Rachel isn't writing she loves to read and spend time with the family. You will often find her with her Kindle, by the pool during the summer, or on the side-lines of the soccer field in the spring and fall or curled up on the couch during the winter months.

She currently lives in Colorado with her extremely understanding husband and their two very supportive children.

Signup for Rachel Ann Smith's newsletter for updates on new releases and monthly giveaways.
www.rachelannsmith.com

Printed in Great Britain
by Amazon

12391560R00140